The
FLEDGLING
HANDBOOK
101

P. C. CAST

with KIM DONER

The
FLEDGLING
HANDBOOK
101

ST. MARTIN'S GRIFFIN
NEW YORK

THE FLEDGLING HANDBOOK 101. Copyright 2010 © by P. C. Cast with Kim Doner. All rights reserved. Printed in the United States of America. For information, address St. Martin's Press, 175 Fifth Avenue, New York, N.Y. 10010.

www.stmartins.com

Book design by Jonathan Bennett

ISBN 978-0-312-59512-8

First Edition: November 2010

10 9 8 7 6 5 4 3 2 1

marked \:märkt, :mákt\ *verb* **1. a:** the act of spontaneous placement of an outlined crescent moon tattoo on the forehead of a human teenager, signifying the beginning of a physiological and sociological metamorphosis which culminates in either vampyrism or death <Suddenly . . . and the tracker reached out and — her—P. C. CAST>

To my high Priestess of Art, Kim Doner:
Thank you for your talent, your hard work,
and your friendship.

—P. C. CAST

Dedicated in honor of beloved consort
Sir Balvin Thorfinnsson,
Knight Extraordinaire and Savior of the North,
Iceland, 968-1016 A.D.

May we find each other
again and again . . .

Within chaos lies opportunity.

–Shekinah, High Priestess of Vampyres

SAN CLEMENTE, ITALY

CONTENTS

The
FLEDGLING
HANDBOOK
101

ABOVE: The first of the Ten Runes is a roughly drawn figure with a hand clasped across the chest, a sign of introduction and/or greeting. By the 11th century, our prehistoric Runes were often manifested as stained glass windows in a House of Night doorway. Presented by the Haus der Nacht, Frankfurt, Germany, 1085 A.D.

INTRODUCTION

MERRY MEET, FLEDGLING. Welcome to a new life, a new world, and a new you. Welcome to the House of Night! Within the pages of *The Fledgling Handbook 101*, you will be introduced to the rich history of vampyres, the foundations of several Major Rituals, as well as the many faces of Nyx, and, finally, you will be awarded a beginner's look at the biological miracle that is the Change.

This is not a rules manual. Quite simply, you are no longer a human teenager. You are a fledgling, which means you are now held to a higher standard of behavior than human young. Fledglings do not steal, lie, or cheat. While we, your vampyre elders, do understand all young people make mistakes, the consequence for consistent fledgling misbehavior is to be expelled from the House of Night. Please refer to the biology chapter for the end result of not being included within a vampyre coven. You may contact the professor of your new homeroom for handouts specific to your House of Night's class hours and lists of elective choices, as well as curfew and cafeteria schedules.

Class Emblems

Each House of Night has its own unique style of uniform, which reflects the school colors and the style of dress decided upon by that individual school's Council, but regardless of where you are attending a House of Night, there will be certain constants agreed upon throughout our society. The schools are all set up on a four-year secondary-education model, with the classes of third former, fourth former, fifth former, and sixth former following the basic freshmen, sophomore, junior, senior—or 9th- through 12th-year grade structure. So that you may more easily navigate your way through your new school, it is important that you understand the class emblems that differentiate the levels of fledglings, as well as the symbology that designates a vampyre as one of your professors. Please study the following insignias and the explanations about them to avoid embarrassment and confusion when you are interacting with teachers and fledglings from upper classes.

OPPOSITE: 14th C. ruin walls of the Tigh ne Nocht near Aberfoyle, Scotland. One of the most historic Houses of Night, this castle enrolled vampyre fledglings from the area known today as the United Kingdom. When the Black Plague struck, vampyres fled for their lives, abandoning homes to hide for nearly a century. Iron plates marking the class emblems were pried from keystones and preserved, as well as wall hangings and illuminated manuscripts.

ABOVE: An early marker for dormitories of the newly initiated, from the Tigh ne Nocht, 14th C., Scotland. All plates presented by Tigh Dhu Museum, Edinburgh.

Nyx's Labyrinth. The Third Former insignia has altered little over time; the design always incorporates gathered energies from the four directions in a central joining. Although a simple spiral has also been acceptably used, a more accurate depiction of Nyx's Labyrinth is shown on the next page.

Third Former

Description: This emblem is called Nyx's Labyrinth and it is a pattern of delicately embroidered spiral pathways, which circle in glittering silver thread just over a third former's heart. Nyx's Labyrinth symbolizes the circular nature of life and the beauty of our belief that though all bodies must die, life itself is eternal and never-ending.

ABOVE: *Nyx's Labyrinth*. These designs were submitted to the Handbook by the HON in Sydney, Australia. They are used as embroidery patterns for school uniforms, often seen on riding gloves, scarves, wraps, and jackets. Many more HONs have adopted their series of emblems.

ABOVE: The Tigh ne Nocht, 14th C., Scotland, Tigh Dhu Museum, Edinburgh.

The Wings of Eros. The design element has remained the same, however, the original carvings made for designated plates had greater emphasis on the wings forming a heart, probably due to the challenges of the medium. With the advances in embroidery techniques, the wings have become more elaborate and a spiral has been added inside each core curve.

Fourth Former

Description: This emblem is signified by the lovely golden wings of Eros, who is Nyx's child and the personification of love. It is meant to remind us of our Goddess's great capacity for love, as well as our continuous movement forward on our individual life paths.

THIS PAGE: *The Wings of Eros*. Digital embroidery design, 2010. By permission of the HON, Sydney, Australia.

ABOVE: The Tigh ne Nocht, 14th C., Scotland, Tigh Dhu Museum, Edinburgh.

Nyx's Chariot. Some interesting changes have happened in the evolution of this emblem. Over the years, the chariot has become more ornate, possibly signifying a belief in the stability of Nyx's children after the trying years of the Black Plague. The body language, indicating a calmer ride with greater control by our Goddess, currently reflects serenity as opposed to rescue in earlier centuries. Stars are now fewer in number, limited to five: four years as a fledgling, and the anticipated move of ultimate proximity to Nyx: the Change into an adult vampyre.

Fifth Former

Description: This emblem is that of Nyx's golden chariot pulling a trail of shining silver stars. The chariot illustrates that you are continuing on Nyx's journey. The stars symbolize the magick and splendor of the two years that have already passed.

THIS PAGE: *Nyx's Chariot*. Digital embroidery design, 2010. By permission of the HON, Sydney, Australia.

ABOVE: The Tigh ne Nocht, 14th C., Scotland, Tigh Dhu Museum, Edinburgh.

The Three Fates. Another shift in history created a new design: scissors became more sophisticated, and are very contemporary in the scene above. To suggest the mystery of the Fates, figures became cloaked in a processional composition.

Regardless of its design, the stark reality holds for all vampyre fledglings as it has before time was recorded. We do not know why one fledgling successfully makes the Change while another does not; it is a mystery yet to be revealed.

Sixth Former

Description: This is the most provocative of the four emblems. Intricately embroidered gold and silver threads bring alive the Three Fates, who are also the children of Nyx. Atropos, the third sister, is holding scissors to symbolize the end of your years at the House of Night. For many of you this will mean the beginning of a long life as a vampyre, though for some of you the scissors of Atropos will hold a darker meaning.

THIS PAGE: *The Three Fates.*
Digital embroidery design,
2010. By permission of the
HON, Sydney, Australia.

ABOVE: *The Tigh ne Nocht*, 14th C., Scotland, Tigh Dhu Museum, Edinburgh.

The Dark Daughters. This plate was located over a fireplace in a small room off the castle's kitchen. There, it is assumed Dark Daughters and Dark Sons held their ceremonies every full moon; the stone floors of the ruins have gaps where beams once stood to support pedestals used for the candles in casting circles.

Although a number of other beliefs also hold the crescents and full moon as important symbols, vampyres initiated the tradition. A crescent is the fledgling, a full moon is an adult vampyre, and the reflected crescent represents a vampyre's journey to fulfill her greatest gifts.

Dark Daughter Symbol

Description: The Dark Daughters and Sons is an exclusive House of Night organization made up of the best and brightest of our fledglings. The Leader of your school's Dark Daughters is a High Priestess in Training. Being invited to join this prestigious organization is a great honor. The symbol for the Dark Daughters is the triple moon, with a full moon in the center and two crescents back-to-back against it. The Leader of the Dark Daughters wears a triple moon pendant outlined in garnets.

ABOVE: *The Dark Daughters.* Digital embroidery design, 2010. By permission of the HON, Sydney, Australia.

ABOVE: The Tigh ne Nocht, 14th C., Scotland, Tigh Dhu Museum, Edinburgh.

Nyx and Her Crescent. The simplicity of the original plate lent itself to a physical response: touch. Adult vampyres in Scotland had a tradition upon entering their halls of learning—to reach up and slide their fingers around the crescent and down the outer arms of the figure as they thanked Nyx and asked for her blessings.

Professor Symbols

Description: Your professors wear one of the universally recognized signs for Nyx. Whatever country you are in and whichever House of Night ends up being your home, your professors will proudly display this emblem. The symbol is as simple as it is exquisite—the fair form of our Goddess, hands raised, cupping the crescent moon.

AT RIGHT: *Nyx and Her Crescent*. Digital embroidery design, 2010. By permission of the HON, Sydney, Australia.

Fledgling Curriculum

This varies for each individual House of Night, but should you transfer to a different HON upon realizing particular talents and affinities, there will be no penalties.

We believe fledglings are most likely to benefit, regardless of if and when the Change ensues, through education that is thorough, dynamic, and challenging. This commitment developed several hundred years ago as new attitudes launched the Renaissance movement in Western Europe, and continues to expand in today's world. So your classes will reflect this: integrated body, mind, and spiritual health will be emphasized at all times.

Most schools begin at 8:00 P.M., and continue until 3:00 A.M. or later, depending on individual interests. Below is a standard school evening schedule, with a variety of classes offered for each former year:

7:45 P.M. Assemblies, general announcements

8:00 P.M. Sociology, Archeology, Philosophy, History

9:00 P.M. Literature and Poetry, Writing, Art: 2-D and 3-D

10:00 P.M. Music, Drumming, Voice

11:00 P.M. Economics, Business, Math, Computer Sciences

12:00 A.M. Lunch: all organic foods, an assortment of local produce and cheeses, red and white wine

1:30 A.M. Foreign Languages, Sciences: Anatomy, Physiology, Botany, Chemistry, Quantum Physics

2:30 A.M. Exercise: Horseback Riding, Fencing, Pearl Diving (in coastal HONs), Yoga and/or Tai Chi, Parkour (in urban HONs), Interpretive Dance, Warrior Training*

After-school activities may include, but are not limited to, the following:

Dark Daughters and Sons gatherings, Priestess-in-Training sessions, shadowing Sons of Erebus Warriors, Feline Enrichment (includes maintenance, exercise, brushing, multiple forms of play, gardening catnip plots, etc.).

HON Media Centers are open at all times. We encourage our fledglings to take full advantage of this, and indulge in any and all literary pursuits.

HON Computer Centers are state of the art and we are currently in the process of installing 3-D studios as well as individual room monitors for our students. Laptops are available for use on and off campus.

Entertainment: All dorms have wide-screen televisions, each fully equipped with high-end technology for the transmission and enjoyment of movies and video games. We have found no need to restrict these options, as most fledglings find our curriculum so engrossing, they have little interest for passive pastimes.

---

* There is the possibility of a young male fledgling displaying early signs of a Warrior Spirit. In these cases, every effort will be made to enhance such development. If/ when his Change occurs, he can then be transported to an appropriate HON facility for Sons of Erebus training, which will be discussed later in the book.

Notes

THIS BOOK BELONGS TO: _____

Date of Marking: _____

Cell phone: _____

HOUSE OF NIGHT LOCATION: _____

City, State, Country: _____

Postal code: _____

Telephone: _____

ROOMMATE: _____

Roommate's date of Marking: _____

Name of roommate's familiar, if so graced: _____

MENTOR: _____

Mentor's cell phone: _____

Name of mentor's familiar: _____

OPTIONAL:

In case of emergency, call: _____

Important numbers: _____

CLASS SCHEDULE

M: _____

_____

_____

T: _____

_____

_____

W: _____

_____

_____

Th: _____

_____

_____

F: _____

_____

_____

AFTER-SCHOOL ACTIVITIES: _____

_____

_____

_____

ABOVE: Haus der Nacht, Frankfurt, Germany, 1085 A.D. The
second of the Ten Runes represents the convergence of life
energies into a center, shown here as an internal spiral.

CHAPTER ONE
Vampyre Biology

INTRODUCTION: Many fledglings find this chapter frightening. Let me begin by reassuring you. Fear can only be vanquished through knowledge and confidence. This chapter exists to educate you about the physiology of what is happening to you. Our goddess, Nyx, exists as loving comfort for you. Be confident that she understands your fear. Seeking her presence and guidance will be a benefit to you long after you have Changed, or have left this realm to join the goddess in the Otherworld.

Physiology of Being Marked

Becoming a vampyre is a complex physiological event that begins when a young adult is Marked some time after puberty, and the sapphire outline of our Goddess's crescent moon appears on the forehead. The appearance of the Mark is a symptom of a biological event that has begun within the body. While we understand the event originates within DNA during hormone surges triggered by puberty, we do not understand why only a small percentage of teenagers are Marked, and why even a smaller percentage of those Marked actually complete the Change to full-grown vampyre.

What we can tell you, Fledgling, is what to expect as your body moves through the metamorphoses which will culminate either in Changing into an adult vampyre, or your death.

ABOVE: Canadian HON, 2004. This young lady's "peek-a-boo" pose serves well to illustrate physical changes a fledgling can expect. Here, she is a normal teenager, three days prior to being Marked by a Tracker. Having been immediately taken to the House of Night by her family upon Marking, she later found this photograph was on her cell phone.

Initial Symptoms

You have already experienced the prequel to being Marked. You felt as if you had a cold with fever, chills, and coughing. At this time your body secreted an invisible essence from your apocrine glands called an Alarm Pheromone that is only present at the very beginning of this sequence of reactions. Left on your own, you would have died within a very few days. Fortunately, our Goddess has gifted a sect of vampyres, called Trackers, with the ability to scent Alarm Pheromones. As soon as you were in the presence of a Tracker, the Preservation Pheromone that only a Tracker secretes began to act on your T-Cell receptors to slow down the degeneration of your pulmonary capillary system. The external evidence of this physiological reaction is the crescent that instantly ap-

THIS PAGE: Canadian HON, 2004. Six weeks into being Marked, she took a similar photograph. Note the differences in eye color, lash length, brow thickness, and skin texture. Hair becomes more reflective and often takes on a variety of shades. Nail beds have altered in shape. Her tattoo is soft and indistinct. This will change as she does, since crescents continue to develop throughout a vampyre's existence.

peared on your forehead.

But, Fledgling, as you well understand, the Tracker's Preservation Pheromone creates only a temporary respite from the potentially fatal reaction that began in your body, which is why all newly Marked fledglings *must* make their way directly to a House of Night so that the Shield Pheromones secreted by all adult vampyres bathe your pulmonary and capillary systems to minimize the unavoidable damage that takes place within you as your body attempts to assimilate the necessary changes that happen in order for you to evolve to the superior physiology of a vampyre.

ABOVE: Canada HON, 2008. Four brief years later, she completed the Change. Her crescent tattoo has sharpened; her eyes have attained their full color, and her skin "glows." (Vampyres are difficult to photograph in daylight, due to mutated surface cells.) Her nails have begun a typical growth pattern with the center of the nail bed laying down a greater thickness at a faster rate. The result is a sharp, pointed tip. This particular fledgling has an affinity for earth, with strong support of environmental energies and an appreciation of the rhythms in life. Interpretations of developing tattoos will be discussed in later Handbooks.

Permanent Symptoms

As you move through the years at the House of Night, and your body continues to adapt to its changing physiology, you will first begin to notice that your hair will thicken and lengthen, your skin will become smooth and clear, your fingernails will strengthen and lengthen.* Your strength, especially in male fledglings, will increase, as will your stamina. Tolerance to temperature changes in your environment will increase. Due to your rising internal body temperature, fledgling males will become sterile and females will stop menstruating. You will also be aware of a change in your dentation. It is, of course, a ridiculous myth that vampyres have fangs, but your teeth will be straighter and stronger than human dentation. You might also begin to notice a change in your saliva. Many fledglings describe this as suddenly being aware of tasting sweetness or tartness. Do not let this disturb you. It is a perfectly normal reaction to the coagulants and anticoagulants that are developing in your salivary glands.** Along with growing fangs, it is also a myth that vampyres cannot bear sunlight. The truth is that our bodies become hypersensitive as they Change, which makes direct sunlight uncomfortable to our skin and our eyes. We can tolerate the light of day, though we prefer the magickal veil of night.

---

*Fledgling, we are not barbarians, nor are you any longer human teenagers. Please maintain proper manicures and pedicures, and overall hygienic maintenance.

**At this time it is not necessary for you to know all the intricacies of feeding on human blood. That will be covered in upper-class handbooks and classroom studies.

Psychological Symptoms

In order to fully understand why these changes are happening to you, you must realize that the Change to vampyre is biologically based on a predator/prey survival system. This is not to infer we are violent beings with uncontrolled urges and evil intent. It simply means that our evolution is based on changes that promote survival in a world where humans vastly outnumber vampyres. This translates psychologically into a more focused intellectual being. So do not be surprised that as your physiology develops and becomes more fully vampyric, you also begin to realize it is easier for you to focus on academic pursuits. Many fledglings discover new intellectual talents and abilities, which often include what humans call a sixth sense.

ABOVE: Canada HON, 2008. A photograph in candlelight, then another when the light is extinguished. Night predators share immediate clarity of vision with vampyres.

Special Notes

Imprinting

It is forbidden for fledglings to feed directly from humans. For your first years at the House of Night this shouldn't be a problem for you to avoid. Typically, your desire for blood only increases as you move closer to the Change. However, we acknowledge that some fledglings do maintain communication with humans, which might lead to experimentation and, accordingly, to an inadvertent Imprint developing between a fledgling and a human. We cannot emphasize enough the dangers of this. Not only are you not prepared for the responsibility of such an intricate physiological bonding process, but the unavoidable fact is that some of you will die. When a vampyre dies, her human consort*** is adversely affected, often to the point of death. Further information about Imprints will be available to you when you become upperclassmen.

***Consort is the official title of a human Imprinted with a vampyre.

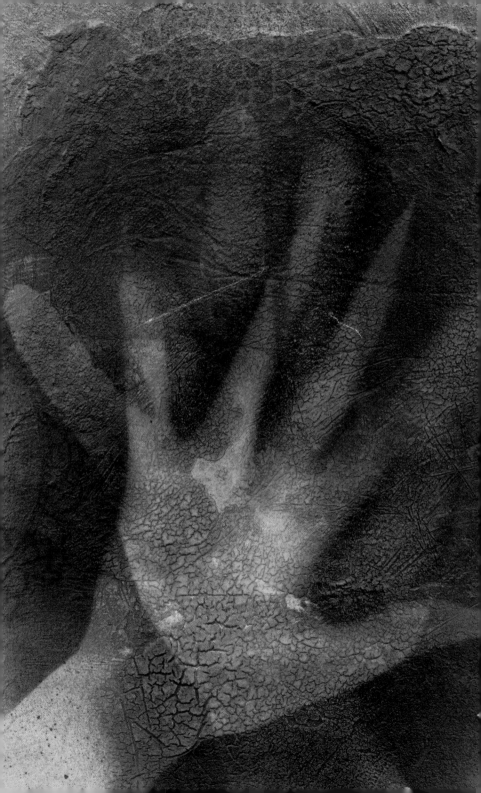

The Warrior Bond

It is also forbidden for a fledgling to accept the Oath of a Warrior. You will learn more specific information about this magickal bond as you progress at the House of Night and move closer to the possibility of completing the Change. As a third former, what you need to understand is that the bond between an oath-sworn Warrior, who must be a fully Changed vampyre, and his High Priestess is more intimate than an Imprint, and more lasting than even that of a relationship with a mate. Because the bond is the result of an oath that is based on protection, an oath-sworn Warrior's spirit will often become intertwined with his High Priestess, and he may develop the ability to sense her feelings. The Oath of a Warrior is to be treated only with the utmost respect and solemnity. It is never to be given or accepted lightly because it is a life-altering bond.

OPPOSITE: France, Grotte de Gargas, 20,000 B.C.E. From the Cave of Mutilated Hands, a prehistoric artist and vampyre expresses the bond with her Warrior. Often used as a signature, artists would blow paint through a reed to create a negative of their own hands, much like small children do today in school. Her Warrior is missing the third finger of his left hand, as do many other hands in this cave. The reason remains a mystery.

Death

Fledgling, it is an inescapable truth that not all of you will complete the Change to adult vampyre. Please understand that during your years at the House of Night, you will witness the death of fellow classmates. Prepare yourself. Once a fledgling's body rejects the Change, there is nothing that can be done to prevent death. You can, however, honor those who do not Change by carrying on and not allowing unavoidable unpleasantness to influence your own development. Know that Nyx will welcome all of her children to her verdant meadows, whether they are fully Changed vampyre or fledgling.

At the right is an early chart for the implications of being Marked, done through our beloved pentagram. As previously discussed, new fledglings *must* enter a House of Night to survive; some do not arrive in time and expire. Sir Richard hypothesized that others do not develop properly, and die. The remaining fledglings who move through the Change, though, are embraced with energies from the merging elements and promised a historically long and abundant life. This is a simplistic version of what is very complex biology merged with the magickal influence of Nyx.

OPPOSITE: Chart by Sir Richard Bowman Cast of Wales, b. 1738, c. 1756, biologist who first recognized the effect of pheromones—termed "influences"—necessary for fledgling survival.

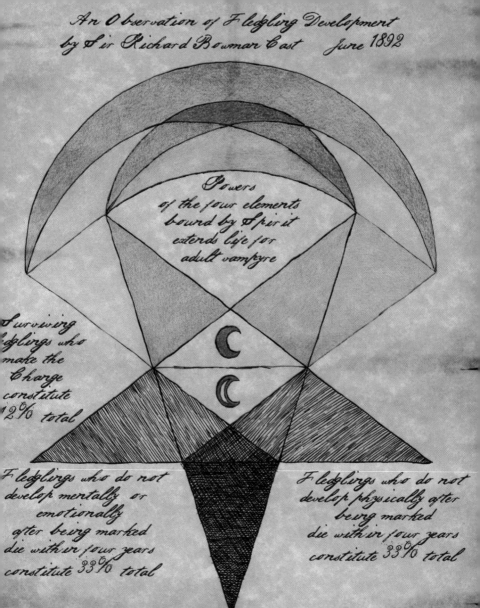

An Observation of Fledgling Development
by Sir Richard Bowman Cast   June 1892

Powers
of the four elements
bound by Spirit
extends life for
adult vampyre

Surviving
fledglings who
make the
Change
constitute
12% total

Fledglings who do not
develop mentally or
emotionally
after being marked
die within four years
constitute 33% total

Fledglings who do not
develop physically after
being marked
die within four years
constitute 33% total

Newly marked fledglings who do not enter a
House of Night expire without influences
from adult vampyres bleed out
constitute 22% total

Conclusion

For as long as vampyres have drawn breath, there has been conflict over the Change. You might know some vampyres who adhere to the philosophy that believes the selection of those fledglings who complete the Change is entirely a random biological act. They will encourage you to exercise and eat well so that your body will be biologically as strong as possible. Others of you will be encouraged by your mentor and professors to focus on learning the Rituals of Nyx, and in being as close to the goddess as possible. Their philosophy hypothesizes that because Nyx grants us free will and the ability to choose our life's path, she is free to choose which fledglings to gift with the Change, and which to allow nature to dominate and destroy. Furthermore, many more vampyres prefer not to enter the debate at all. Whichever is your experience, it is important to focus and understand what we know are indisputable facts about the Change.

OPPOSITE: South Africa, Western Cape, 1200-1000 B.C.E. This cave painting celebrates new fledglings joining the HON when their biological responses, seen as a spiral, draw them into a center of acceptance by Nyx.

Personal Documentation

Fledgling, please complete the left side as soon as possible, and be sure to date your entry. You are creating a history for later comparison as you move towards the Change.

PLACE
PHOTOGRAPH
IN THIS SPACE

NAME: _____

DATE: _____

Physical observations: _____
_____
_____
_____
_____
_____
_____
_____
_____
_____

DATE: _____

PLACE
PHOTOGRAPH
IN THIS SPACE

Physical changes I have noted in the past year: _____

_____

_____

_____

_____

_____

_____

_____

_____

_____

ABOVE: Haus der Nacht, Frankfurt, Germany, 1085 A.D.
The third of the Ten Runes is a bridge, at times indicating
an exchange (in current terms, a "round trip"), other times
suggesting an isolated and life-altering event of no return.
A bridge always means a choice.

CHAPTER TWO
Rituals

INTRODUCTION: Rituals are the heartbeat of vampyre society. They are how we exalt Nyx. They are also how we mark many aspects of our lives. Vampyre society has Major Rituals, which include but are not limited to moon phases, changes of season, group cleansings and protections, the death of a familiar, the breaking of an Imprint, the celebration of Samhain, Yule, Beltane, and Eostre.

Though rituals differ according to the talents, preferences, and needs of each individual High Priestess, there are some aspects of Ritual that do not change. There is always a Circle cast before Ritual commences.

When casting the circle, the High Priestess will always begin in the east and call air to her. She will then move clockwise, or deosil, around the circle, pausing in the south to call fire, west for water, north for earth, and finally moving to the middle to call spirit to complete the circle.

Candles are usually lit in each of the five directions as the element is called. The following colors are used for the candles: air—yellow, fire—red, water—blue, earth—green, and spirit—purple.

NORTH: Earth, the fourth element, joins and invites spirit to fill the circle.

EAST: The first direction, where air begins the circle.

WEST: The circle deepens with water's addition.

SOUTH: Fire responds and its energies curve into the spiral.

When the ritual is completed, it is customary for the High Priestess to close the circle by thanking each of the elements in turn as she moves counterclockwise around the circle, ending where she began in the east with the element air. It is important to remember to maintain a focused mind and positive thoughts during Ritual, and to ground yourself with food, drink, and relaxation after Ritual. Note that blood is often used in Ritual, but rarely for fledglings younger than sixth formers.

To begin to understand the importance of Ritual, you must familiarize yourself with the historical foundation of five of our most sacred rites. So, Fledgling, turn the page, and with it let time fall like scales from your eyes. Prepare yourself to be enchanted by some of our most glorious High Priestesses and the rituals they inspired.

ABOVE: Calcutta, India HON, 2001, where fledglings integrate their culture into the HON by decorating a table with the saris worn for their first Casting.

ABOVE: Haus der Nacht, Frankfurt, Germany, 1085 A.D. The
fourth of the Ten Runes is a combination of three crescents
to form a flying figure, signifying trust and fearlessness.
However, like air, these beliefs are transparent to others and
can be abused by them if displayed too quickly.

The Dark Daughters' Induction Ritual

Element–Air

The origins of the Dark Daughters can be traced to the year 60 A.D. in Briton. At that time the most prosperous Celtic tribe was the Iceni, led by the courageous human queen, Boudicca, who refused to bow to Roman rule. To teach the Iceni queen a lesson in submission, a Roman tax collector, Catus Brutus, had the defiant Boudicca publicly whipped, and forced her to watch while her two teenage daughters, Mirain and Una, were brutally raped.

Though only a human, Boudicca showed the courage of a vampyre Sons of Erebus by donning battle garb and rallying the Celts against the mighty Roman legions. History books record her army's short-lived victories, their eventual defeat and slaughter by the Romans, as well as the fact that Queen Boudicca committed suicide shortly after her army was slaughtered.

But human history reports nothing of what happened to her daughters . . . and that, Fledgling, is because vampyre history tells their story.

After the tragic battle, both girls were Marked. Weak and ill from being newly Marked far outside the protective boundaries of a vampyre coven, the brave lasses made their way through their war-ravaged land to the Scottish Highlands and the House of Night on the Isle of Skye.

There they grieved so fiercely for their mother that the vampyres had little hope their fledgling bodies would accept the Change, and so the coven left the girls to their mourning, almost as if they were afraid to catch the contagion of their misery.

Utterly alone and believing they would be forever heartbroken, the girls had no desire to live. In the stillness that comes with the very end of the night, they made their way to the edge of the cliffs at Neist Point, determined to hurl themselves to their deaths and thereby rejoin their beloved mother and queen.

And then Air stirred.

THIS SPREAD: *Una and Mirain's Last Moments.* c. 1970. House of Night: Hall of Priestesses, Tulsa, OK. By consent of the Southwest Vampyre Council, USA.

Carried by the salt breeze through the roiling mist of the Isle, Nyx's voice was heard by Mirain and Una. Just before sunrise, in the glooming that signals the beginning of dawn's rosy fingertips ascending the sky, the goddess's voice, filled with a mother's love, came to them wrapped within an elemental affinity offering them a new life.

"Oh, my dark daughters, you are so filled with despair that it grieves me deeply! Do not throw away your precious lives! Be brave and embrace this element and your new destiny. Know that I am ever with you. Listen with your hearts and you shall hear me in the breeze that leaps at your call. Look with your souls and you shall see me in each other's eyes. My love for you is as eternal as the air you breathe, and over which I grant you control. I ask that you choose life, love, and happiness. Let me heal your sorrows so that you might find strength in each other, my beautiful, brave, dark daughters . . ."

The element air filled the sisters with the love of the Goddess, and as Mirain and Una heeded Nyx's words and accepted their new destiny, her compassion healed the sisters' broken hearts. There, facing the sea and the dawn, for the first and only time in vampyre history, fledglings Marked for a mere fortnight Changed.

Before they left the jagged cliffs, the newly Changed vampyres swore a sacred oath that they would never allow another fledgling to feel the lonely despair that had almost cost them their lives.

They sealed the oath with the power of wind.

They swore the oath to Nyx.

They bound the oath with the words *"The dark daughters choose life!"*

Thus the Dark Daughters were born.

BELOW: Una and Mirain's legendary tattoos, as interpreted from ancient scrolls. Their symbols show a deep affinity with Air, and many have been repeated on other Priestesses once their bonds have developed. c. 1970. House of Night: Hall of Priestesses, Tulsa, OK. By consent of the Southwest Vampyre Council, USA.

Dark Daughters' Induction Ritual
Element–Air

Before casting the circle, the Leader of the Dark Daughters should personally place a small table made from the wood of a Silver Fir, which is also known as a Birth Tree, in the center of the circle area. The Leader should arrange three yellow bowls on the table around the purple spirit candle that always rests at the center of a cast circle. Fill one bowl with dried basil leaves, one with fresh saltwater, and one with the dried needles of a Silver Fir. She also needs to fill a Ritual chalice with mead.*

Then the Dark Daughters' Leader should decorate the table with items of her choosing, which represent the element air, as well as things that symbolize friendship. For example: She might choose feathers to represent air and brightly colored ribbons braided together to represent the intertwining of friends' lives.

When the table is made ready and the circle cast by the Leader of the Dark Daughters, the candidate for induction is called to the center of the circle. The Leader dips her fingertips into the bowl of saltwater and sprinkles it around the candidate saying:

"In memory of the sea-bound Isle of Skye where the Dark Daughters were born, I use saltwater to cleanse the space around my sister candidate."

---

*Mead was a favorite drink of the ancient Celts, and in using it during the Dark Daughters' Induction Ritual, you are honoring Mirain and Una. Please note that some fledglings mix blood with the Ritual mead. That is not encouraged unless upperclassmen are being inducted.

ABOVE: SIR RONALD FLEMING. 9th C. A.D. Bruges, Belgium. Hand-cast leaded crystal chalice. Gifted to the HON for Dark Daughters' exclusive use in their ceremonies when his daughter was Marked and Changed during adolescence. Presented by the Flanders Vampyre Collection, Belgium.

The Leader returns to the table and, with the spirit candle, lights the bowl of dried basil. After the flame is sufficient to produce smoke, she blows it out. With gentle hand motions she encourages the breeze to carry the basil smoke to the candidate, who should breathe deeply. As the smoke wafts over the candidate the Leader continues:

"Sweet basil exorcises negativity. As air carries basil around and through you, let any negatives be banished from your life."

Returning to the table, the Leader lights the dried fir needles with the spirit candle. These, too, should be blown out after the flame is sufficient to produce smoke. Holding the smoking bowl before her, the Leader should walk slowly around the candidate three times, saying:

"Be brave and embrace your new destiny. You know that Nyx is ever with you. Now, from this day forth, know that your sisters, the Dark Daughters, are also ever with you. If you are afraid, call on wind for a sister, and you will be answered. If you are lonely, go to a sister and you will know friendship. When you look in the eyes of another Dark Daughter, know that you see the love and compassion of Nyx reflected there."

The Leader returns to the table for the chalice and offer it to the candidate, saying:

"If you accept the pledge of this sisterhood, you will never truly be alone. What is your choice, Fledgling?"

The candidate should then take the chalice, hold it up, and joyfully proclaim:

"I choose life!"

And as she drinks deeply from the chalice, the Leader and those who have witnessed the Ritual shout:

"Welcome to our sisterhood of life, love, and happiness! Welcome, Dark Daughter!"**

The new Dark Daughter is honored by being allowed to close the circle. Afterward food and drink should be shared in celebration. Many Leaders gift the new member with a special present to symbolize the Dark Daughter's birth into the sisterhood.

Cleopatra's Protective Ritual

Element–Fire

It is well documented by human history that Cleopatra was the only Pharaoh of Egypt who was also a Vampyre High Priestess. Human historians record that she was Marked four years before her father, Ptolemy XII, died in August of 51 B.C., and that the day he was entombed she completed the Change.

Ptolemy XII left his vast kingdom to his son, Ptolemy XIII, but decreed he must rule jointly with his sister, Cleopatra, and that—according to ancient Egyptian tradition—the brother and sister must marry.

**Male fledglings are, of course, welcomed by the Dark Daughters and are called Dark Sons during and after the ritual.

ABOVE: Haus der Nacht, Frankfurt, Germany, 1085 A.D. The
fifth of the Ten Runes reflects the release of passion, tempered
with a warning: if motives are pure, all will be well. If motives
are from a negative source, beware.

OPPOSITE: Cleopatra's tattoos, as interpreted from Egyptian
hieroglyphics. The oft-mentioned asp was a symbol of power
and is seen centered in the headdress of Pharoah. Here, it
curves into the back of her crescent. c. 1970. House of Night:
Hall of Priestesses, Tulsa, OK. By consent of the Southwest
Vampyre Council, USA.

But Cleopatra was no longer human, and she was too wise to blindly follow an abhorrent tradition. She did leave the Thebes House of Night to return to Alexandria, though she had no intention of marrying her brother. Human texts tell that she used Julius Caesar and the power of Rome to banish her brother–how she eventually married Mark Antony after Caesar's assassination–and how her love affair with Mark Antony led to Egypt's downfall and her death.

Once again, we must look to vampyre history for the real story.

In Egypt Nyx is worshipped as Nyx-Sekhmet, which translates literally as Goddess of Night and Fire. Even before she was Marked, Cleopatra left offerings of incense and sweet oil at the Temple of Nyx-Sekhmet in Alexandria. Her scrolls, preserved by the Thebes House of Night, explain in her own words how being Marked and then Changed felt natural to her. Cleopatra recounts how her dedication to Nyx-Sekhmet had so deepened during the four years it took her to Change, that the High Council declared her High Priestess status immediately. She was destined to become a powerful voice on the Vampyre High Council, but her father's death and her decision to leave vampyre society to rule Egypt irrevocably altered her fate.

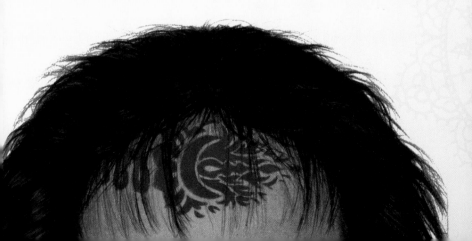

Cleopatra Encircles Alexandria.

c. 1970. House of Night: Hall of
Priestesses, Tulsa, OK. By consent of
the Southwest Vampyre Council, USA.

Before facing the Egyptian nobility, the newly Changed Cleopatra retreated to the desert outside Alexandria, where she spent three days and nights fasting and praying to Nyx-Sekhmet, beseeching the Goddess to aid her in her determination to rule Egypt without being forced into an abhorrent marriage with her brother. The Goddess was moved by Cleopatra's love for the Egyptian people, and she answered the young vampyre's prayers by gifting Cleopatra with an affinity for fire that was so powerful that when she emerged from the desert and entered the city, the Egyptian people were awestruck at the sight of her.

The ancient vampyre historian Seshat describes the scene:

And behold! As the sun set in the west, Cleopatra entered Alexandria. The vampyre blazed. Her thick dark hair had taken on a bronze sheen and, thus gilded, it lifted around her burnished shoulders in response to the power that flamed from her body. She was a golden goddess of fire. Even her dark eyes had taken on the color of fire, for they glowed an unearthly amber.

The people cried out that she must be Nyx-Sekhmet-Come-to-Earth, but Cleopatra did not claim the Goddess's divinity. In a voice amplified ten times she cried, "I am not She, but I have been touched by Her flame, and if you accept me as your one true Pharaoh,

*I will use the power of fire to protect you for as long as
I draw breath!"*

    *Alexandrians, commoners as well as nobility,
bowed willingly to Cleopatra, banishing her brother
when he tried to insist they must follow human
tradition and marry him to his sister.*

    *The day they crowned Cleopatra Queen of Upper
and Lower Egypt, she called upon her element, fire,
and publicly cast a protective circle around the city of
Alexandria, which held her people in safety for the
next two decades . . .*

Ah, Fledgling, I can imagine your confusion. You are won-
dering why Cleopatra's Protective Ritual is of such importance
if it only lasted two decades. Your answer is that the focus here
is not Cleopatra's ritual, but in the lesson learned through its
deterioration.

Julius Caesar was, indeed, an ally of Cleopatra and Egypt,
which is only logical as he Imprinted with her during his first
visit to Alexandria. The great vampyre pharaoh even visited
Caesar in Rome, and she mourned the loss of her consort
deeply when he was assassinated by power-hungry humans.

Mark Antony, too, allied himself with Cleopatra after Imprinting with her and becoming her second consort. It was
this Imprint and Mark Antony's desire to forsake his home-
land and live at Cleopatra's side that turned Rome against
Egypt.

Rome demanded Mark Antony's Imprint be broken, and that he return to resume his position as Commander of the Legions. Cleopatra refused to be parted from Antony saying, *"Rome has taken one consort from me. They shall not have another!"*

The Egyptian nobility begged Cleopatra to reconsider. They said the kingdom could not stand against the might of Rome.

Cleopatra refused to listen.

The Vampyre High Council took the unprecedented action of becoming involved in human politics. They met with Cleopatra, urging her to remember she was not simply a vampyre in love with her human consort. She was Pharaoh of Egypt and responsible for the safety of a nation of humans.

Cleopatra refused to listen.

Her handmaidens told the commoners stories of how they witnessed Nyx-Sekhmet appearing to Cleopatra within the flames of the Pharaoh's hearth fire, speaking words of reason to her daughter and trying to guide her back to the right path.

As you have learned, Fledgling, our Goddess's greatest gift to all of her children is that of free will.

Cleopatra chose not to listen.

Rome came against Egypt, and while Cleopatra was paralyzed with fear for her consort, she forsook her people, and the protective circle around Alexandria crumbled from a flame of power to ineffective ash. The city was invaded. Mark Antony attempted to lead the Egyptian army and stop the destruction, but Cleopatra's fear for him had taken away his warrior spirit, and he was killed. The Egyptians were enslaved.

Upon learning of Antony's death, Cleopatra called to her element and commanded it to cleanse her of the unbearable grief and guilt she was feeling. Like a giant serpent, fire consumed the vampyre, swallowing her whole.

So you see, fledgling, the importance of a Protective Ritual is not found within the circle itself, but is instead found within the vampyre who casts it. Let the memory of Cleopatra guide you to wise choices . . . .

A Protective Fire Ritual

Note: The following is a Ritual used to cast protection over a House of Night, though fledglings should note a Protective Ritual may be used for many different purposes, ranging from something as broad as the protection of a campus or a city, to something as specific as protection of a mate or consort.

In order to perform an authentic Protective Ritual with a fire emphasis, the priestess conducting the ceremony must follow Cleopatra's guidance and seclude herself, fasting and praying, three full days before the night of Ritual. It is not necessary for the priestess to retreat into a desert for her seclusion, though she should be utterly alone—speaking to no one except Nyx. During this time, the priestess should set her Ritual Intent. This means she must focus on what or whom it is she wishes to protect and why she feels the need for the Ritual. Remember, fledgling, it is through the priestess that the protection will succeed or fail. Should her intent be honorable, and should it remain that way, the Ritual will succeed, though to what extent depends entirely upon the strength of the priestess. Add even a shade of dishonorable or selfish intentions, and the Ritual will become as ineffective as oil in putting out fire.

A Protective Fire Ritual begins exactly at dusk on the third day of the priestess's fast. The circle should already be prepared for her, with candles at each of the five element stations, and witnesses assembled around the circle. In the center of the circle on a wrought-iron table, there should be a red chalice filled with precious oil mixed with cinnamon. As the sun sets, the priestess should enter the circle without speaking. She should be carrying long wooden matches* and an athame.**

The priestess casts the circle and then goes to the oil-filled chalice. Holding it before her, she should begin at the east and walk deosil around the circle, pouring the oil into her right hand, and with that hand, sprinkling the oil around the circumference of the circle. As she walks, she says:

> *"I call upon the element fire to watch, bless, and guide this Ritual. To honor fire I anoint the circle with cinnamon oil poured by my own hand and I proclaim my Intent to seek the element's protection over this House of Night. To show my Intent is pure, I proclaim these ancient truths first spoken long ago when Cleopatra, another child of Nyx, called upon you."*

---

*Modern lighters should never be used when evoking the aid of fire in any Ritual.

**An athame is a knife used only for Ritual.

OPPOSITE: *Ceremonial Knife*. 250–200 B.C.E. 10", gold. From the Collection of Fatima Bastet, Cairo Gallery of the Night, Egypt.

In a loud, clear voice the priestess should cry,

"Hail, Nyx Strider! Coming forth from seclusion I have done no wrong. Hail, She-Whose-Two-Eyes-Are-on-Fire! I have not defiled the things of the Goddess in thought or deed. Hail, Disposer-of-False-Speech! I have not inflamed myself with rage. Hail, All-Seeing-Goddess-Provider-of-Her-Children! I have not cursed using Your name."

The ancient proclamations end when the priestess returns to the center of the circle. She lights the oil left in the chalice and holds it over her head saying:

"With pure Ritual Intent I hold fire to this oath of protection. Its strength is in me and through me its flame will be lasting, consuming with fierceness any who wish ill to this House of Night."

Still holding the flaming chalice, the priestess then takes her athame and approaches the yellow candle that represents fire at the east edge of the circle. Passing the blade through the chalice flame three times, she says:

"I am one with the flame. Even in the midst of sunshine, I enter into the protective fire, I come forth from the fire, the sunshine has not pierced me, thou who knows my pure intent has not burned me, but thy fire will keep this House of Night safe, cutting like this knife through wax any who dare to defile this Ritual."

With the hot athame the priestess should carve the name of her House of Night into the yellow candle, and then carefully place it in the chalice, allowing the flame to consume it. While it burns, she should thank the other elements and send them away, and the witnesses should also go quietly, leaving the priestess alone with the burning candle. She should wait until the entire candle is consumed and the flame dies of its own accord before she leaves.

This Ritual is very draining for the officiating priestess. Afterward she must re-energize*** as well as ground herself.

Circe and the Full Moon Ritual

Element–Water

The Full Moon Ritual is unique in its purpose. It is the only Major Ritual that exists solely to enable vampyres and fledglings to know the beauty and enchantment of Nyx by transcending the boundaries of the physical world. Out of all the exquisite High Priestesses who have led this ritual, there is one vampyre whose memory outshines the others. The following is lovingly dedicated to her.

Until the month of August in the year 79 A.D., the Vampyre High Council made its home on the lovely island of Capri. Many extraordinary Vampyre High Priestesses reigned there, but the most widely recognized of our ancient home's matriarchs was Circe, to whom Nyx gave the gift of an affinity for water. It was Circe who Imprinted with the famous traveler, Odysseus, and Circe who inspired the building of Pompeii. Such was her beauty and allure that ancient artisans crafted Pompeii to be *"A jewel so exquisite it might aspire to adorn the bosom of Circe."*

***You will learn more information pertaining to how vampyres re-energize if you become a sixth former.

ABOVE: Haus der Nacht, Frankfurt, Germany, 1085 A.D.
The sixth of the Ten Runes is a rough depiction of seven
water droplets tumbling together, curving in motion. The
Water rune represents fluidity, creative flow, solutions and
connecting; its dark side can indicate instability and madness.

Of course Circe was more than just a beautiful High Priestess. She walked Nyx's path and was so devoted to the Goddess that she could find the magic of Nyx's touch in even the simplest of things.

Humans feared her and labeled her witch and sorceress, creating an entire mythology about her long and magick-filled life. Vampyres adored her and called her goddess-blessed. When she passed over to the Otherworld, it is said the aquamarine blue of the Mediterranean surrounding Capri turned black for three days in mourning for her.

Of all Circe's talents, vampyre historians agree that she was most adept at drawing down the full moon. We know this to be true not just from vampyre legend. Today portraits of Circe performing Full Moon Rituals can be found gracing the walls of many national museums including: the Louvre, the British National Portrait Gallery, and New York's Museum of Natural History.

Perhaps one of the reasons Circe's moon rituals were so extraordinary was that she had the ability to foretell the exact date the full moon would crest between the twin Faraglioni Rocks just off the southern coast of Capri. Of the Faraglioni, Circe wrote:

All around my rocky beauties the azure sea reigns
supreme, caressing the Faraglioni with a salty kiss.
One of my darlings appears sculpted as if by Nyx's
hand, with a fantastic inlay tunneled through its core.
The other juts proudly from the coast, like a sentinel

Warrior—ever vigilant, ever aware. And when our
Goddess, in the form of a glowing silver moon, is
drawn between them, magick ensues . . .

Now, Fledgling, prepare to be gifted with a unique jewel.
The text that follows has been translated from the only surviving ritual written in Circe's hand from her personal journal.
Here, in the long-dead High Priestess's own words, behold the
magick of a Capri Full Moon Ritual.

The Full Moon Ritual

Element—Water

The following was translated from the High Priestess Circe's
personal journal:

> *I could feel it coming in the air tonight, though it wasn't*
> *until after dusk that I knew beyond any doubt that the*
> *tumescent moon would crest between the proud jut of the*
> *Faraglioni rocks this very night.*
>
> *As befitting an event that happens, at the most, twice a*
> *year, the High Council instantly spread the word, signal-*

ing with the beacon fire on our rocky outcropping and calling all vampyres within sight home to Capri.

My priestesses prepared me, taking special care to anoint my body with fine oils, to outline my eyes with kohl, and to dress me in the richest of my Ritual garb—a sheath so soft it felt as if I was wearing a garment made of water turned to cloth through the magick of Nyx.

I chose the largest and most beautiful of the conch shells I had collected during the last full moon. I held it carefully before me while the priestesses and Sons of Erebus escorted me from the castle to the winding path that led down to the southern shore. As we walked, I saw that the light from their torches reflected the pink center of the shell as if illuminating a secret.

Should I live an eternity I will never forget the joy of this night. When the warm sea, ripe with salt and life, touched my bare feet, I thought I might faint at the wash of pleasure that filled me.

Ah, Goddess! You so richly blessed me when you gifted me with water! As always, I praise your name!

Had the moon not been hanging full and bright between my beloved Faraglioni, I could have stood there for

OPPOSITE: Circe's tattoos, developed over centuries by her philanthropic leadership along the Amalfi coast. Note: Inside her crescent can be seen a chambered nautilus, one of her favorite animals and a living form of our spiral. c. 1970. House of Night: Hall of Priestesses, Tulsa, OK. By consent of the Southwest Vampyre Council, USA.

hours, utterly charmed by the sea. But the Goddess's moon reminded me of my purpose so, with the aid of four favored priestesses, I lit each of the element candles, placing them in turn on the hollowed pieces of driftwood carved specially to hold them. When my circle was complete, the music began. Drums beat, flutes trilled, and cymbals shimmered with happiness made audible. Those gathered lifted their voices in sweet harmony, and I danced, filled with the sea and the silver light of the moon. When that glowing orb was high enough in the sky, I raised the conch, signaling the music to quiet, then I launched the small candle vessels, stepping deeper into the embrace of the sea with them.

As always, my circle remained complete. My element did not fail me. Out of love for me, and to honor the Goddess, tides and waves stilled, suspending motion so that I stood with my conch in the center of a magickal circle.

Smiling, I dipped the shell into the sea and then turned to face the multitude that stretched as far as I could see along the shore and up the rocky coast.

"Merry meet!" I cried.

"Merry meet!" Their response was a joyous shout.

"The full moon is a time when the veil between our world and the Goddess—the known and the unknown—is transparent. On nights such as this, magick is afoot!"

OPPOSITE: *Circe Calls Down the Moon.* c. 1970. House of Night: Hall of Priestesses, Tulsa, OK. By consent of the Southwest Vampyre Council, USA.

I spoke the words I knew so well that it seemed as if they had been written across my heart. "Tonight Ritual takes on a layer of mystery as the glistening symbol of Nyx has risen between our beloved Faraglioni. So tonight, vampyres, we revel in the Goddess's additional blessing. Any task you finish tonight will be blessed . . . any purpose you choose to voice tonight will be blessed . . . any joining you wish to complete tonight will be blessed."

"Hail, Nyx!" they cried.

"And now, I shall finish this Ritual of magickal completion."

I turned so that I faced the full moon, shining so brilliantly that it caused the Faraglioni to cast deep blue shadows over the water. Holding the conch above my head, positioned so beams of silver light made the water within it molten, I recited the Full Moon Blessing for my people:

"Above me I feel your love
    my Goddess
Full of the promise that through you
    my Goddess
All things ripen and come to fruition
    my Goddess
As the diaphanous boundary between worlds
    my Goddess
Is illuminated by the white light of your sign
    my Goddess
I ask that some small ray of your love descend
    my Goddess
Fill this seaborne chalice
    my Goddess
So that I might pour it over me
    my Goddess
And take your gentle touch to the children of the night."

I could not see the water within the conch, which I still held over my head, but I knew the instant Nyx's hand

OPPOSITE: CIRCE. Full Moon Blessing. 8th C. B.C.E. Imported papyrus and ink. Presented by the Napoli La Casa di Notte, Italy.

touched it by the sudden warmth that radiated through my palms and the joyful gasps I heard echoing along the shore.

"The Full Moon is blessed for all to see;
as the Goddess wills, so mote it be!"

I shouted the words as I poured the goddess-filled water over my head and down my body. The water covered my skin until I glowed with a silver light that so mirrored the moon that I had to close my eyes so as not to be blinded by its brilliance, and while the priestesses closed the circle, I rejoiced with Nyx's children of the night through song and dance, laughter and praise, and above all else through love . . . always love . . . .

ABOVE: Photograph submitted by Sofia da Este, a sixth former fledgling who lived in Sorrento, Italy, prior to her Marking. Once Changed, she returned to her coastal home to host a Full Moon Blessing; look closely to see the light of the shell's glow upon the dancing vampyres.

Spirit Release of a Familiar

Element—Earth

The lovely city of Beregen, Norway, was founded in 1070 A.D. by the Son of Erebus Warrior, Olav Kyrre. The city thrived, filled with merchants and craftsmen, artists and poets. In 1270 a vampyre High Priestess known as Freya was on a scouting mission to discover a site for a new Scandinavian House of Night, over which she would preside. Her first stop was Beregen, known then as it is now as the gateway to the scenic fjords of Norway's west coast.

Freya was entranced by the city and instantly fell in love with the strong, majestic mountains that spread around Beregen like an amphitheater to the open sea. As a High Priestess whose gift from Nyx was an affinity for earth, Freya rarely felt secure so close to any large body of water, but in the thirteenth century the best form of trade and travel was by waterways, so it seemed Beregen might be the perfect choice for her new school.

But Freya was as wise as she was beautiful. Instead of making such an important decision impulsively, she retreated deep into the Norwegian forests. Secluding herself so that she could be surrounded by only the wildness of the land, Freya centered herself, cast a sacred circle, and then prayed earnestly to Nyx, asking that the Great Goddess send her a sign if Beregen was truly the correct choice for the new House of Night.

ABOVE: Haus der Nacht, Frankfurt, Germany, 1085 A.D. The seventh of the Ten Runes depicts the two directions a tree grows: upwards and outwards, towards the sky, and down to extend in the dark, a metaphor of how greatest strengths are also greatest weaknesses.

Immediately Freya heard a voice echoing through the boughs of the pine trees saying:

If my forest children accept you, then you have made the right choice, daughter.

As the echo faded into the trees, two enormous cats padded out of the forest. Though rarely seen, and almost never domesticated, the High Priestess recognized that her visitors were Forest Cats of Scandinavian legend.

It is not known exactly what happened between Freya and the cats, whom she named Kaia and Kaira, but over and over again artists and storytellers have recreated the dramatic scene of the slender, graceful High Priestess emerging from the forest, flanked on each side by a majestic Norwegian Forest Cat. Her hands resting on each of their noble heads, the three seemed one. The local humans cried out in fear that she must have bewitched the beasts, but Freya laughed and said, "*It is I who have been bewitched—by these wondrous creatures and by your delightful city!*"

Human history reports that Freya's open joy, her tawny beauty, which so extraordinarily complemented the Forest Cats who had chosen her as their own, and her obvious connection to the land won over the populace. The humans of Beregen were able to overcome their superstitious natures; they embraced the new House of Night, and it was built with the aid of local craftsmen on a spectacular mountainside location overlooking the city. Freya and her Norwegian Forest Cats became so popular with the people that the High Priestess had a special chariot crafted for the cats, and she could often be

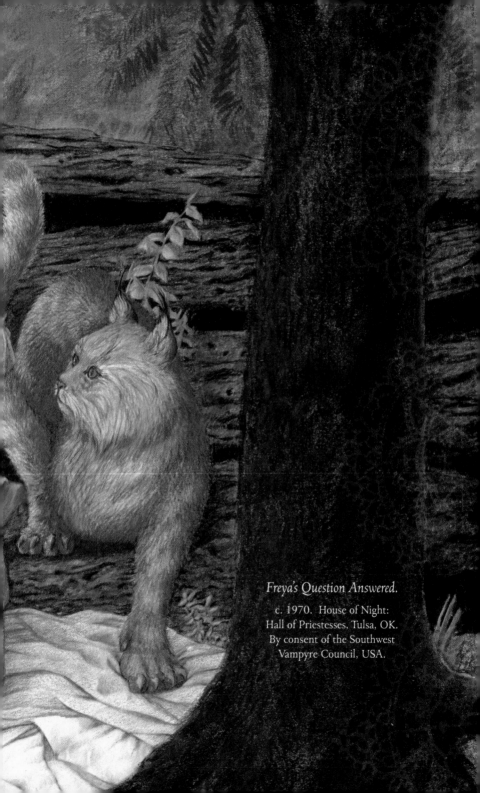

Freya's Question Answered.

c. 1970. House of Night:
Hall of Priestesses, Tulsa, OK.
By consent of the Southwest
Vampyre Council, USA.

seen riding through the narrow, winding streets of the city, being drawn by her beloved Kaia and Kaira.

The two Forest Cats lived an unheard-of half a century, and died within the same hour of each other. They were so loved by everyone at the House of Night and in the city that, at the death of the cats, for one of the few times in recorded vampyre history, a High Priestess allowed non-Imprinted humans to take part in a Major Ritual: Spirit Release of a Familiar.

Fledging, if a cat chooses you as his or her own, you will be richly blessed by your feline's devotion and love. When you lose your feline, as they all must cross over to the Goddess's Otherworld much sooner than will their vampyres, be prepared for your grief, and know that even after death, your feline will still be devoted to you. Thus it is important to ritualistically say farewell to your feline's spirit, so that she will be free to frolic, kittenlike, in Nyx's meadows and not be trapped in this world, lonely and incorporeal, unable to truly be with you, yet also unable to allow her spirit to depart.

The following Spirit Release of a Familiar Ritual is based on records of Freya's farewell to Kaia and Kaira. It is heavily influenced by the earth element, which is especially important when releasing a spirit. The vampyre should stay well-grounded to the earth, but the dead must be ruled by spirit to be fully released from this realm.

Spirit Release of a Familiar Ritual

Element–Earth

This Ritual is best performed outside in an area as unpopulated by humans as possible, and should take place within three days of the feline's death. This is one of the few Major Rituals that does not have to be performed by a High Priestess, but should instead be led by the vampyre who has lost his or her feline. To honor the bond between cat and vampyre, everyone attending the Ritual should bathe and dress in beautiful robes before they come to the circle.

On the table in the center of the circle should be representations of the cat: pictures, her favorite toy, an offering of a special food she liked, etc., as well as a braided rope of sweetgrass and a white sage smudge stick. Inside the circle in front of the earth candle there should be placed a green bowl filled with cream.

After the circle is cast, the vampyre leader should light the sweetgrass braid. Walking deosil around the table, she should waft the smoking braid through the air saying:

"_____(insert the name of the deceased cat), *with equal parts love and sadness I call you to me one last time.*"

The vampyre should continue calling her feline until she feels the cat's spirit presence. At that time it is appropriate

OPPOSITE: Freya's tattoos, from descriptions found in her writings. These are very direct: flowers, vines, trees, and animal prints to represent the bounties of the earth. c. 1970. House of Night: Hall of Priestesses, Tulsa, OK. By consent of the Southwest Vampyre Council, USA.

for the vampyre to pause the Ritual and reassure the little cat spirit that she is still greatly beloved, and will never be forgotten. These words should be very private, unique to each cat, and though they are not a scripted part of the Release Ritual, they are necessary and important. After the vampyre feels she has reassured her cat's spirit, she should then light the smudge stick and continue saying:

"As a child of the Goddess, I know that when a being dies, the soul lives on. That dying is only a way of forgetting pain and suffering—that it is a pathway to travel back to the God-

ABOVE: 13,000–12,000 B.C.E. Serra da Capivara, Brazil. The vampyre-familiar bond had ancient beginnings. In this cave painting, a vampyre hunts with the now-extinct *Smilodon populator*, commonly known as a saber-toothed tiger.

dess to be renewed and made strong—to rest and to one day be ready to return to this realm, for it is spoken by the High Priestesses thus:

> *Arrayed in a new body another mother may someday give birth so that with stronger limbs and brighter mind the old soul shall take the road to earth again.*

But for this belief to be made reality, you cannot languish here. You must depart this realm to join Nyx in the Otherworld."

The vampyre should walk to the northernmost part of the circle and stand with the smudge stick in front of the lighted, green earth candle. Breathing deeply of the cleansing sage, she should smudge herself, from toe to head, and then using the smoking sage as a wand, the vampyre must trace our sacred pentagram* in the air before her three times as she recites:

> *"Small friend, I thank you for the years of love and laughter you gave me. Small friend, I will hold your memory in my heart always. Small friend, I ask you now to forget your broken shell and your worries for me. I bid you in the name of Nyx to pass from this realm, to go beyond, to rest and to enjoy frolicking in the meadows of the Goddess."*

---

*The pentagram is a five-sided star sacred to the Goddess's children. It is not, as human culture has misidentified it for years, a sign of evil. The pentagram is simply a sacred symbol of the five elements: the upper point representing Spirit, and the other four points representing Air, Fire, Water, and Earth. We wear the pentagram with the Spirit point up to symbolize the eternal aspect of our souls and the path we walk which will some day lead us, in spirit form, to our Goddess.

The vampyre should then pour the bowl of cream in a circle around the earth candle saying, "*With this offering to the earth and with love and the fullness of my memories, I release you and bid merry meet, merry part, and merry meet again!*"

The vampyre and those in attendance must then visualize a shining door just outside the northernmost part of the circle. As one they need to imagine the glowing door opening to reveal a beautiful meadow filled with waving grass, and the small, bright spirit of the cat leaping joyfully through the door, which closes softly behind her.

The Ritual is then complete. Often one of the vampyre's close friends will close the circle, allowing the vampyre the opportunity to spend those moments grieving and remembering . . .

ABOVE: D. E. ENGLAND. Farewell, Chenise. Early spring, 2006. Photograph, 8X10". Tulsa, OK. By permission of the vampyre. Author's note: this photograph was chosen for the reminder of hope—new grass shoots coming through the snow.

The Amazon High Priestess
and Herakles: Breaking an Imprint

Element–Spirit

The Amazon warriors of ancient Asia Minor, in what is known today as Turkey, have mystified humans for thousands of years. They are not mysterious to us, Fledgling, because we know exactly who the Amazons were, where they lived, and what became of them.

The Amazons were a group of vampyre priestesses who chose to live separately from all men, even vampyre males. It is documented by the Vampyre High Council that in the first century B.C., a priestess named Hippolyte approached them with a petition signed by twenty-five vampyres, requesting that they be allowed to withdraw from society and make their own coven—free of male influence. The Council granted the priestesses's request, and even aided Hippolyte and her women in establishing their isolated settlement off the coast of the Black Sea, high in a rugged mountain range known as the Amazonians at the site of the Spring of Thermodon.

There the priestesses lived in utter freedom. They continued to be faithful in their worship to Nyx, but other than the Goddess, they answered to no one except Hippolyte, who they chose to call Queen and not High Priestess. They were expert equestrians and fearless warriors who dedicated themselves to training in the arts of archery and the use of the deadly doubled-sided battle axe. Legend says they even tamed the

ABOVE: Haus der Nacht, Frankfurt, Germany, 1085 A.D.
The eighth of the Ten Runes represents all energies and all
directions, a simultaneous flow of connection between what
can be physically experienced, or measured, and what is
qualified within: the spirit.

majestic tigers of Asia Minor, who were as devoted to them as are our beloved felines today.

But the Amazons, as they became known, caught the attention of the Hellenistic Greeks. Heavily patriarchal, the Greeks could not bear the thought of women existing without men. So a Greek king, Eurystheus, sent his greatest hero, Herakles, to steal from Hippolyte her golden breastplate. Knowing the violation would cause the women to take up arms to defend themselves, the Greeks planned to let the Amazons strike the first blow, and then they would slaughter them in retaliation.

Fledgling, this is not the first nor the last time humans have underestimated vampyres.

Herakles did make his way to Thermodon, but he was surprised when he and his men were welcomed graciously by the Amazons. Hippolyte herself ordered a banquet feast for their guests. The vampyres danced and sang and celebrated with an unrestrained joy that intrigued Herkales and his men. Never before had they seen women so powerful and beautiful and alluring. That night, Herakles invited the raven-haired Hippolyte to drink from him, which was when the Amazon Queen and the greatest hero of the Greeks Imprinted.

You see, Fledgling, the Amazons did not hate men. They simply wanted to live free—on their own terms—owing allegiance only to their Queen and to Nyx. They chose to be their own warriors, workers, helpmates, and companions.

For the next two months, Herakles didn't leave Hippolyte's side. By day they galloped horses through the treacherous mountain passes and matched each another, arrow for arrow, on the archery range. By night they loved each other completely.

But their contentment was only temporary. As the two months came to an end, Herakles revealed to Hippolyte his king's hidden agenda to send him to steal her golden breastplate and provoke a war between the Amazons and Greece. Upon hearing this news, Hippolyte smiled, went into her chamber, returned with her golden breastplate, and gave it to Herakles saying:

> *"You cannot steal a thing with which you have been gifted. There will be no war, as that would not be Nyx's will, nor would it be good for my women. So, take this gift to your king, along with my deep affection for you, my brave, beautiful Greek warrior."*

Now remember, Fledgling, Cleopatra has already taught us a lesson about the dangers of a vampyre becoming overly infatuated with her consort. You also need to understand that it can be as equally destructive if a consort becomes obsessed with his vampyre.

Herakles replied that he would not return to Eurystheus. Instead he would stay there, by Hippolyte's side, for the rest of his life.

The Amazon Queen's reaction was shock and dismay. She did not falter. She insisted that Herakles return to his world, where he belonged, explaining to him that she had thought he understood the bond between them was only temporary, that the two of them could not be together in this lifetime as she, along with her women, had pledged to live lives free of men.

Human mythology spins a wild tale to cover up what followed Hippolyte's rejection of their hero, but the story of the bloody battle between the Amazons and Herakles's men, and the report that Hippolyte and her women were slaughtered, is only fiction. The truth is that the great Greek hero had to be bound by his own men and dragged from the Amazon Queen's camp, and that as he was carried away, he shrieked oaths, swearing that he would return and reclaim her love.

Hippolyte thought she knew what she must do, but before taking action, she isolated herself for three days and nights, praying to Nyx, who came to her in a dream at the end of the third night. The Goddess simply nodded once and said three words, *"Yes, my daughter."*

The Queen returned to her women, knowing that she was, indeed, on the right path. She explained that she believed the Greeks would not be satisfied to leave them in peace once her rejection of Herakles became public knowledge. So they would have to leave the wild beauty of Thermodon and become spirits themselves. If they wanted to remain free, they

OPPOSITE: c. 1970. *Hippolyte and the Infinity of Spirit.* House of Night: Hall of Priestesses, Tulsa, OK. By consent of the Southwest Vampyre Council, USA.

must disappear into the wilderness of Asia Minor, never to be seen again by human or vampyre.

Before they left, Hippolyte had to complete two tasks. First, she sent an Amazon rider to the High Council so that their story would be told before she severed all contact with vampyre society. Then, to ensure Herakles could never track her through their blood bond and lead the Greeks to them, Hippolyte performed a Ritual to Break an Imprint.

And then, the Amazons disappeared forever.

Human mythology records Herakles did not survive for long after Hippolyte broke their Imprint. The myth says a poisoned cloak killed him. Vampyres un-

TOP LEFT: This heart crystal was given to Hippolyte by Herakles as a sign of his adoration, and safely stored for centuries by the HON in Greece. Photograph courtesy of The Athens Museum of Ancient Vampyre History.

BOTTOM LEFT: *Hippolyte.* 1250 B.C.E. Marble bust, approx. 30". Photograph courtesy of The Athens Museum of Ancient Vampyre History.

OPPOSITE: *Hippolyte with her familiar, Korku.* c. 1970. House of Night: Hall of Priestesses, Tulsa, OK. By consent of the Southwest Vampyre Council, USA.

derstand that the poison was in his own mind, and the cloak was symbolic of his inability to allow his love to be free.

If you have the good fortune to complete the Change and become a vampyre, remember to consider wisely before you choose a consort.

Breaking an Imprint
Element–Spirit

Note: After careful consideration and much discussion, the Vampyre High Council, led by Shekinah, made the decision to remove this Ritual from *The Fledgling Handbook 101*. Apparently, the inclusion of the actual Ritual led some fledglings to believe they could feed from humans without fear of Imprint, because should the Imprint happen, they could simply turn to this text and reverse it.

Fledgling, Imprints are many things, but they are *never* simple.

Though it is rare for a fledgling to have the ability to Imprint, it can happen; therefore, we cannot impress upon you strongly enough the fact that an Imprint is a soul-altering bond. It should never come about as a result of experimentation or irresponsibility. It changes the human and vampyre/fledgling irrevocably. Breaking an Imprint is a painful, shattering experience.

Human consorts have been killed when the vampyre with whom they Imprinted has been injured. Human consorts have also died as a result of their vampyre purposely breaking their Imprint, as evidenced in the example of Hippolyte and Herakles.

It is unspeakably cruel to subject a consort to a Ritual Imprint Breaking for frivolous reasons and the High Council, our Vampyre High Priestess, and the governing Council at your House of Night will not tolerate such barbarity in their fledglings. Accordingly, the details of this dangerous Ritual have been moved to the *Fledgling Handbook 401*, which is made available only to those fledglings who are at the end of their House of Night journey and in their sixth former year.

As a lesson about consequences, we decided to include in your handbook the story of Hippolyte and Herakles, in which the consort died after his vampyre willingly severed their Imprint, and the Amazon High Priestess, along with her people, were forced to disappear from our world so completely that only legend and lies remain of their brave, bright culture.

ABOVE: *Shekinah, the Mother Tree*. A commemorative tile created sometime in the sixth century to celebrate the Change of a new priestess. Photograph courtesy of the Archives of Shekinah, Tiberius, Israel.

First Circle experience: _____
_____
_____
_____
_____

Possible affinity element? _____
_____
_____
_____
_____

How did you know? _____
_____
_____
_____
_____

My first Familiar: _____
_____
_____
_____
_____
_____
_____
_____
_____

PLACE
PHOTOGRAPH
IN THIS SPACE

High Priestess at our House of Night: _____

_____

Vampyre professors and their affinities or gifts: _____

_____

Air: _____

_____

Fire: _____

_____

Water: _____

_____

Earth: _____

_____

Spirit: _____

_____

_____

Anyone unique to this House of Night: _____

_____

Strengths I am now recognizing in myself: _____

_____

_____

_____

ABOVE: Haus der Nacht, Frankfurt, Germany, 1085 A.D.
The ninth of the Ten Runes represents the divergence of life
energies from a center, shown here as an external spiral.

CHAPTER THREE
Nightkind Elementology

Most of you are already familiar with the human system of western astrology where the zodiac sign under which a person is born determines much of his or her personality. In 200 A.D., the vampyre Polemy found validity in this system, though he observed that it wasn't so much the *sign* under which a person was born that informed their character traits as it was the *element* that corresponded with the sun sign. At that time he approached the Vampyre High Council with a hypothesis thus stated:

> *If humans are affected at birth by the element of their astrological sign, then it seems a logical assumption that vampyres would be similarly affected by the sign under which they Change, as the Change from human to vampyre is truly a rebirth.*

The High Council was intrigued by Polemy's theory and charged him with creating a new system of classification for vampyres, based more heavily on the elements than on the astrological sun signs.

In 300 A.D., after one century of observation and research, Polemy presented to the Vampyre

High Council *Nightkind Elementology*, wherein he assigned an element to correspond with the date of a vampyre's Change. The attributes of the specific element are what molds and informs the maturing vampyre's character traits. Polemy expanded the human's four element astrology system to include our culture's fifth element, spirit. For the select few who complete the Change during what he titled the *ascension of spirit phase*, they are ruled predominantly by spirit, but will be influenced by the overlapping element.

The following is an introductory version of Polemy's Nightkind Elementology sign chart. In it you will find elemental influence dates, a short list of some of the major character traits, and elementology symbols. After you complete the Change, you may delve further into your element of influence. For now, Fledgling, simply consider: Under which element do you believe you will Change?

Air

If you Change between December 1st and February 28th, you are influenced by air.

A vampyre influenced by air elementology will tend to be: freedom-loving, idealistic, unfettered by small thinking, have excellent communications skills, be charming, unselfish, and noble.

Fire

If you Change between June 1st, and August 31st, you are influenced by fire.
A vampyre influenced by fire elementology will tend to find it easy to express her inner nature. They are enthusiastic and vibrant, and require acknowledgment and approval to experience contentment.

Water

If you Change between September 1st and November 30th, you are influenced by water.
A vampyre influenced by water elementology will tend to adapt easily to changing environments. They get things done through the power of their emotional commitment, and are gifted with the ability to rechannel negative feelings and experiences into constructive activities.

Earth

**If you Change between March 1st and
May 31st, you are influenced by earth.**
A vampyre influenced by earth
elementology will tend to be: sensual,
pleasure-seeking, well-grounded and
emotionally secure, nurturing, and
creative. They are goal-setters who love
to see their plans come to fruition.

Spirit

If you Change during any of the following days spirit influences you, but you will also be affected by whichever element it overlaps.

Spirit Elementology days are:

FEBRUARY 1, 2, 3	MARCH 20, 21, 22
APRIL 30	MAY 1, 2
JUNE 20, 21, 22	JULY 31
AUGUST 1, 2	SEPTEMBER 20, 21, 22
OCTOBER 30, 31	NOVEMBER 1

A vampyre Changed during Spirit Elementology days will tend to be: a charismatic speaker, self-assured, highly intuitive, multi-talented, passionate, and intense.

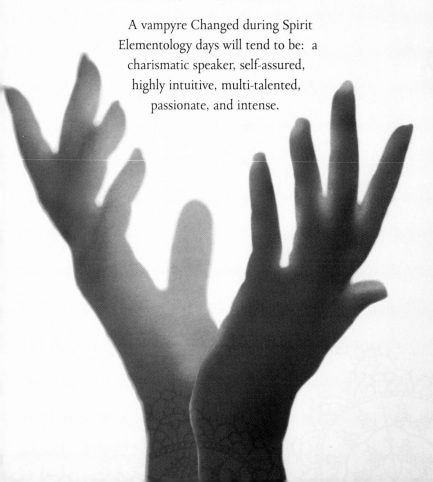

Celebrations

These are universally held for the Houses of Night, as vampyres travel extensively to renew old ties, enjoy holidays, and maintain close connections with each other. Many Houses of Night have their own local events as well, so please ask and note to stay current.

PRIMORIS VAMPYRA. JANUARY 1 (for third formers) means "first vampyre" and, for one day, role reversals occur as new fledglings are allowed all privileges given upper classmen and professors while they assume the roles of new fledglings.

IMBOLIC. FEBRUARY 2

PLURIMOS DILIGO. FEBRUARY 14 (for fourth formers) means "most loved" and all forms of caring are shown to their greatest degree within each House of Night.

EOSTRE. MARCH 21

CARITAS NYX. MARCH 30 (for fifth formers) means "Nyx's chariot" and is usually a competition of ancient games. The games vary within each House, due to geography and weather.

BELTANE. APRIL 30

SUMMER SOLSTICE. JUNE 21

FAUTOR PER FORTUNA. JULY 21 (for sixth
formers) means "favored by fate" and is a formal
blessing for them. This event invites human family
to join residents of the House of Night as they unite
and send combined energies to sixth formers as
their day of Change grows near.

MABON. SEPTEMBER 21

SAMHAIN. OCTOBER 31

TERMINUS BELLUM. NOVEMBER 23 - A time to
acknowledge our history and give thanks to Nyx for
the end of the Vampyre Wars.

YULE, OR WINTER SOLSTICE. DECEMBER 21

ABOVE: Haus der Nacht, Frankfurt, Germany, 1085 A.D. The
tenth of the Ten Runes incorporates the sign of a familiar
within the hand of a vampyre. Besides meaning a cherished
companion, the rune is also used for that which is known,
intimate, and recognized.

CHAPTER FOUR
A Brief Introduction to Vampyre History

VAMPYRES HAVE ALWAYS EXISTED. We have walked the earth as long as grass has grown, the sun has shone, and the moon has turned in its elliptical orbit. While we do have a written history better preserved and more ancient than humans, we did not gather as a society until the ninth century B.C. It was then that a unique vampyre High Priestess named Lilith emerged from the fertile region known as Mesopotamia. Lilith was greatly gifted by Nyx, having an affinity for spirit, as well as the prophetic ability to envision the final threads of a vampyre's life. Using her goddess-given gifts, Lilith called together the High Priestesses of every major vampyre coven, along with their consorts and warriors. She persuaded her sisters and brothers to form what she titled the Vampyre High Council—a ruling body that would be the center of all vampyre peoples. In it she, along with the seven leaders of the major civilized vampyre covens, set about creating the standards of our unique and beautiful society, wherein women are held sacred, as is the worship of the Goddess, and men are appreciated and respected.

Lilith and her new Vampyre High Council debated long about where they should make their home. They knew it must be a place that was defendable from human invasion and exploitation, but it also had to be near a major seaway for travel and supply. And, of course, it should be a place of beauty and wonder—something that soothed and nurtured our innate love of the earth and the magick of nature.

THIS PAGE: ARTIST UNKNOWN. Watercolor, 18X14", c. 1880–1890. The rendition of a decorated buffalo hide includes the symbol of Nyx and the crescent moon (see inset). USA.

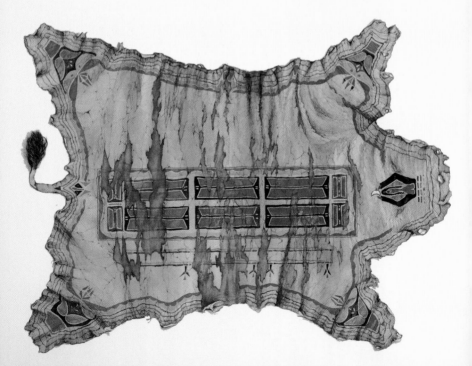

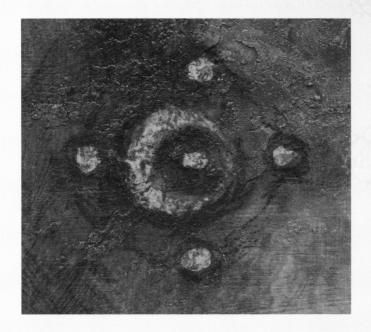

Finally, after much searching, during the eighth century B.C. Lilith and the High Council decided to make the blue island of Capri, off the southern coast of Italy, their home.

In no time, vampyres spread along the exquisite Amalfi Coast, founding and then acting as philanthropic patrons of beautiful Pompeii and Herculaneum, twin cities of light and magick and art. Lilith's own words best describe what our ancient home was like:

> *The Amalfi Coast is a flower-filled garden labyrinth with*
> *Pompeii and its sister Herculaneum at the exquisite entrance*

ABOVE: Lascaux, France. 17,000–15,000 B.C.E. Upper Paleolithic art confirms prehistorical vampyre existence and rituals.

to its maze, enticing with coquettish charms for all to enter,
and Capri is the glistening treasure at its center.

Until August 24, 79 A.D., Capri, Pompeii, and Herculaneum were bound, heart and soul. On that day, tragedy struck both vampyre and human. The great and brooding mountain known as Vesuvius erupted, consuming Pompeii and Herculaneum, and killing so many human consorts that it is said an uncountable number of vampyres lost their lives that day attempting to save their humans from the death that rained from the sky.

The Tragedy of Pompeii

Note: "The Tragedy of Pompeii" was initially told verbatim and passed down from one generation of storyteller to the next. It was finally written down sometime during the seventeenth century and recently translated for this edition of *The Fledgling Handbook*.

Fledgling, we truly hope all of you not only survive but thrive in each House of Night, discovering inner strengths you may never have realized you possessed. Even today, there are still many mysteries surrounding the powers of the vampyre race; our limits are yet unknown. This story is not as old as our kind, but illustrates the many gifts we have been given by Nyx and is, in particular, a legend concerning the misdirection of these abilities.

In 58 A.D., Theodora and Antonia were born to a Pompeiian slave. Their owner was an experienced slave trader. Brutus considered himself a connoisseur of females, and had amassed a fortune through his expertise. He was known as shrewd, and exhibited no hesitation in taking advantage of those who were not.

Brutus followed trends in Rome, Napoli, Florence, and their nearby port towns for the latest entertainments. He trained slaves to meet current popular indulgences, whether as gladiators, chefs, masseurs, or experts in pleasure. Always sensitive to demand, Brutus ensured anything imagined could be found in his stables, were one willing to pay the price. He had moved to Pompeii, reputed for its love of luxury, to pursue fresh income from the more decadent populations.

Among these populations were active and retired military men, and many had joined a new religion: Mithraism, the worhip of the bull. Brutus saw opportunity there, and enlisted as a new initiate (after all, these men were reputed for lusty indulgences and the money to command them). A secretive sect, human art history books depict a white bull being bled, interpreted as a sacrifice. This is inaccurate.

Vampyre scrolls from Capri indicate this bull elicited an ancient, dark power. Members used an elaborately carved knife to wound the bull and drink its blood, bonding to its power much like a malevolent Imprint. Soon after joining, a man became a terrifying fighter in war, returning home with great honor, but in the long term, such cruel energy brought only tragedy and destruction. Brutus had heard that members of this mysterious belief became "more" of whoever they were, too: harsh, aggressive, carnal; he ignored these warnings.

Such men were perfect patrons for a mercenary like Brutus. He understood their drive for constant stimulation and shared their never-sated hunger for the exotic and forbidden.

He wore their knife with pleasure for marketing potential: The handle carved into the shape of a bull clearly showed above his belt.

In Theodora and Antonia, he saw enormous potential. For twins to survive birth was rare, but to grow into such beautiful beings was phenomenal. Matching sets of black, sooty eyes were surrounded by glowing olive skin, and beneath delicate noses, full lips framed pearl-white teeth. With proper instruction, they could someday fetch an enormous sum.

As there was no actual "childhood" in ancient times, training began young. The girls, with their natural grace, were well versed in the arts before their bodies began to mature. Their beauty inspired Brutus with a scheme: sell them to the Mithraists for their virgin blood, then continue to rent them to other patrons who might be intrigued with the idea of enjoying a female previously used by the fearsome warriors.

In historical context, it was frowned upon to abuse slaves, but not prevented; females in particular could be loaned, rented, traded, or sold. Brutus intended to profit in all ways, interviewing likely clients among the Mithraic membership as Theodora and Antonia grew into young women.

Throughout their early years, Brutus carefully maintained a distance; it was foolish to tempt oneself with future pristine merchandise. But as the twin beauties ripened, he found it progressively difficult to ignore them. The idea of keeping the lovely twins for himself also began to work its way into his mind.

Unlike Brutus, the children were embraced by a loving

community, where many believed they were truly two halves of a whole. Never far apart, some said one soul must have cleaved in their mother's womb; Theodora was full of fire, always searching and questioning, quick to anger but quicker to laugh. She reigned in the slave quarters with her storytelling skills and playacting before bedtime. *"Nia, watch me now!"* she would cry, and all heads would turn to see her newest stunt.

ABOVE: *Mithras and the Blood of the Bull.* Artist unknown. Graphite rendering of a famous marble statue carved 300–400 A.D. Rome, Italy..

Her passions were contagious. She could engage even the most curmudgeonly and waspish into long-forgotten forms of childhood play.

Antonia was her opposite: calm, soothing, and kind, her nature healed and comforted. A quiet and melodious voice made her songs achingly sweet. She did not hide behind Theodora; she balanced and reflected her, at times even joining her antics or scrambling to catch up, calling out *"Wait for me!"*

Such a personality is readily seen as easily used, but Antonia was no fool. The kitchen help often sent her to the market to bargain for the best produce and meat. The butcher, known for his stinginess, nonetheless anticipated her visits, even though he knew she would get the best of him. Perhaps it was how she always complimented him in ways he longed to hear: respect, gratitude, and acknowledgment of his experience. He returned home alone each night, her words warming him as he drifted to sleep.

Together, the two complemented instead of competed. Smiles followed the children as they went about tasks in the quarters; their dark, glossy ringlets bounced together and apart as they shared secrets and laughter. More glances of appreciation came their way as they matured into young women.

Brutus began to receive offers for the twins, but curtly

OPPOSITE: *Putti Serving Wine.* 1st C. A.D. Restored fresco, Second Style, Pompeii, Italy. Believed an early portrait of the twin slave children, found in the House of Cherubs. Unlike most, they have dark hair and are fully clothed, a standard set by Brutus to maintain a mystery around the children. From The Pompeii Collection, Hall of History, Venice, Italy.

rejected them all. For the first time in his trade, he had no answers, only an unsettling and ever-growing obsession with the two, for he was as male as any other. Even his Mithraist brothers, whose interest and friendship he had cultivated, were making inquiries. He found himself avoiding their questions.

Then one fateful morning, Brutus awoke to a cry from the slave quarters. Antonia lay curled around her sister, and the usually energetic Theodora lay glistening in her own sweat, pale and limp. The grief-stricken girl told him she had awakened to see a young man, sapphire crescent on his brow, leaning over Theodora, placing a fingertip upon her forehead.

Just before dawn, Theodora had been Marked.

Enraged, Brutus left the quarters. His options had suddenly altered drastically; he no longer had a matched set of nubile young women. One was ensured to either be lost to him as a vampyre, or die in the process. Even more, his own secret fantasy was ruined, and Brutus flushed with anger in realization.

But Brutus thought further. Maybe he could turn this to some advantage. He had been patient all these years; perhaps Theodora could be manipulated on her sister's behalf after joining the Vampyre Palace. With proper promotion, he could work Antonia twice as often . . . or demand her sister join her for sport . . . .

Hours later, Brutus returned to find his servants sitting, flanking Antonia. She wore a glazed expression as she stared into nothingness. He moved forward to shake her out of this trance, but to his astonishment, an elder servant boldly thrust up a halting hand and demanded, "*Leave her be. For now. Leave her be.*"

And, in even greater astonishment at himself, he did as he was told.

The separation of the girls created worthy gossip. Some wondered when Antonia would herself Change. Others suggested Theodora had actually escaped, or been secretly sold to pirates, or that this was a dramatic ploy by Brutus to raise the value of the twins.

Antonia simply lay as if dead in their room. At one point, the cook even checked for a pulse.

In the Palace of Capri, the vampyres struggled as well. Theodora, having been revived by their pheromones, demanded her twin be brought to the Isle to join her. But for centuries, entry to the palace had been forbidden to humans, and for excellent reasons. Vampyres were often seen as a threat by ignorant humans, and past fanatics had manipulated mobs into destroying Houses of Night. Additionally, in ancient times, there had been fledglings who had not controlled themselves accordingly, and Imprinting had occurred with tragic results. Hence, the standard for fledglings had been set, Theodora being no exception. This plunged her into a deep depression, so intense she failed to notice the compassion on new faces surrounding her. Had she studied any, she would have seen one face in particular watching her with the focus only a vampyre can have. He could not take his eyes off of Theodora.

This young vampyre, a recent Son of Erebus, had been a Roman soldier before his Change. His prowess in war had brought him great renown. One battle, in particular, had been recorded and celebrated; he had overcome a Celtic leader, purportedly a powerful druid. Originally a nameless slave, he was allowed by his general to adopt the name of his slain foe: Drusus.

Drusus had entered Capri as a fledgling, but not as an average adolescent. His years as a slave, then as a warrior,

ABOVE: *Antonia and Theodora*. 1st C. A.D. Restored fresco, Second Style. Pompeii, Italy. Brutus promoted the twins by having opposite single ears pierced—Theodora's left ear, and Antonia's right—not only for exotic looks but also for identification. From The Pompeii Collection, Hall of History, Venice, Italy.

had carved his body into art. After the Change, his physique emerged as that of a young god. Muscular arms and legs met in a flawless torso, braced by wide shoulders and topped with a warm smile; arched brows framed eyes the color of the sea. Now Drusus was undergoing another "change," one unique to him but known throughout time to the rest of us. It is called *love at first sight.*

He withdrew from the painful scene as Theodora collapsed in despair against Hestia, the High Priestess of Capri. But the young warrior had a plan. That evening, a boat sailed from Capri, and a bargain was struck with Brutus (probably through some level of powerful persuasion best left unknown). Antonia moved to a small but opulent residence in Pompeii—a private apartment only the wealthy might own. There, Drusus sat and held the hand of Theodora's double. He found himself staring into the thick-fringed, adoring eyes of Antonia as tears of gratitude turned into jewels sliding down her cheeks. Although he felt no masculine urges (as he had with Theodora), Drusus nonetheless knew this human was one he must protect at all costs; she was the other half of the one he loved, and necessary for Theodora to feel whole.

Drusus made a pledge: to be the official courier between the two until Theodora made her Change, believing with his entire heart this would occur. He returned to the palace with Antonia's first message to Theodora.

His promise helped the twins shoulder their painful separation. The potential of their reunion, although possibly years away, kept Theodora hopeful. She excelled at classes and embraced the rituals; Antonia accepted the financial assistance of Drusus and opened a bakery, down the street from a particularly besotted butcher. Drusus, a man of his word, was often seen traveling back and forth with gifts, scrolls, and drawings sent from one sister to the other, some of which have survived the centuries. He stayed a respectful distance from Theodora, but his devotion to her was painfully obvious to everyone save Theodora herself. Even her twin recognized the longing in his eyes when he produced a missive from Capri and held it an instant longer than necessary, simply to touch something of hers. The only shadow during their years of waiting was the threat of Brutus.

Rumors circulated of how the sudden loss of Theodora and Antonia had inflamed his known temper, but the experiences of Mithraic rituals expanded it into chaos. His rages came from nowhere; his employees constantly suffered from the escalating cruelty. Over and over, people heard him muttering one-sided conversations with the missing twins. Slaves became terrified as the false dialogue shifted and signs of madness emerged. Brutus coerced his female slaves to dye their hair, shape their brows, and don the pale-colored tunics left behind by the twins. He walked the night, carrying their abandoned scarves, holding them to his face, inhaling; as time went on, he would withdraw his knife from its sheath and polish it with the same scarves.

OPPOSITE: Drusus. 1st C. A.D. Fresco, Fourth Style. Palace of Capri, Italy. A painting by an unknown vampyre artist of Capri. From The Pompeii Collection, Hall of History, Venice, Italy.

Brutus might have been obsessed, but he was not foolish. He discovered Antonia's whereabouts and often spied from the shadows. He would watch Drusus arrive, then leave before dawn to return home; other times, the vampyre would remain in the apartments until the next day. Brutus wrongly decided Drusus had stolen Antonia for himself, and the thought drove him insane. Somehow, he would retrieve his matching prized possessions; somehow, he would wreak revenge on the vampyre warrior who had taken them from him.

Meanwhile, Theodora had surprised the elders of Capri with how rapidly she grasped and implemented the skills they taught. Their greatest surprise, however, occurred during her first circle casting.

While conducting the ceremony, Hestia felt a surge of Nyx's energy, and glanced about for the source. Her eyes fell on the young maiden, who stood, eyes closed, waves shimmering down her arms and leaping off her fingertips. Theodora slowly stepped into the center of the circle, floating forward like a wraith—the material of her gown billowed about her in unnaturally slow waves, her heavy braids uncoiled from about her head, then unfurled into a cloud around her face. Thick, black lashes lay upon her cheeks as she raised her chin and lifted her hands, palms upwards, receiving an invisible gift. Everything in the circle slowed; some wrote later how a heavy gold comb loosened from her hair and slowly drifted down to the ground. *"Blessed be,"* spoke Theodora, voicing Nyx's eternal promise.

An element had claimed her. Theodora had been chosen to embody Spirit.

The circle ended, leaving Theodora awakened and newly aware. The energy she had previously used to explore the world became internally directed, slowing her, lending depth to thoughts. She viewed her surroundings in a fashion many painters allude to, which is the sense of the eyes experiencing all three dimensions of a subject: not simply at face value, but encircling and *through*, knowing it completely; knowing it intimately. She knew . . . *focus*. She studied her hands, held them before her face, then looked up between them to receive the steady gaze of . . .

Drusus.

Hestia wrote of their profound bonding upon Theodora's recognition of him that evening. Ignoring questions and comments about her display of energy during the circle, Theodora's eyes were on Drusus as she finally understood the longing in his face and surrendered to his magnetic force. They slipped from the throng and fled to the shore of the island. As sounds carried over water, many ducked their heads and smiled to accidentally hear the passionate moments that followed. From then on, they were seldom apart but for his travels to Pompeii on behalf of the twin sisters' exchanges.

Months became years, and the day came when a celebratory circle was cast to ask Nyx's blessings for a newly Changed vampyre. In the gathering, Theodora sank into the trance that elicited her unusual force within Spirit. This time, due to her passage into completion, it was much stronger. Everyone stood, mesmerized, as the flickering candles stilled and motes of dust hung in the air. Moths, wings frozen in flight, cast shadows against the walls, and suspended smoke stopped its lazy drift upwards in a gauzy web about them. Whatever mass she gazed upon became motionless.

When the circle ended, few noticed Hestia's troubled face but she later wrote of her concern for power in one so inexperienced. That August evening, the Isle of Capri celebrated Theodora's initiation, and with great joy, she prepared to finally reunite with her sister. On the twenty-third day, they sailed forth to join Antonia.

Drusus had prepared for this moment. At dawn, as the sun warmed the sky, he knelt before Theodora to offer his warrior's eternal oath. It is said his eloquence and sincerity were as beautiful as the scene itself. With a cry of delight, Theodora accepted his pledge, and the Son of Erebus took the young priestess into his arms as their companions cheered.

The ship approached port as the western sun cast its golden glow upon the figure of Antonia. Ignoring decorum, Theodora flung aside the tent flaps and leapt across the gap between ship and dock to fling herself upon her laughing sister. Words tumbled out as fast as tears of joy fell; the twins embraced, and two halves became whole again.

That evening was the Festival of Vulcanalia, the Roman god of fire, and much was planned throughout the countryside. The populations loved opulence and luxury; lavish parties were held, most notably one being thrown by Drusus to honor Theodora and Antonia. By now, he found it much easier to tell them apart. Living in daylight, Antonia had changed: Her features were etched and her body had a fullness not seen in young vampyres. Still, she was lovely, the mortal reflection of Theodora's near-timeless features. Their many friends toasted them both over and over. Had Drusus indulged as heartily in the flowing wine, he might not have noticed the hovering shadow by the atrium gates.

Brutus had lurked on the other side of the walls, listening to the laughter and stories. Hours passed, his tension mounted—it was all he could do not to tear down the wrought iron gate and reclaim his possessions. How could he destroy Drusus and recapture his slaves?

ABOVE: *Theodora's Trance.* 1st C. A.D. Fresco, Fourth Style. Palace of
Capri, Italy. Hestia's writings refer to this fresco painted by a vampyre
of Capri who witnessed Theodora's first Circle. From The Pompeii
Collection, Hall of History, Venice, Italy.

Immersed in his own bloodlust, Brutus was caught off guard when a hand slammed down on his shoulder. Between gritted teeth, Drusus again used his "power of persuasion" on the trader, who angrily slunk away into the shadows, fingering his beloved knife and muttering *"But they are mine, MINE . . . ."*

The morning sun bled through a strange haze throughout the city. Most residents attributed it to all the parties and fires of the previous night. At the sea gate, the twins' parting was hardly as before: Theodora and Antonia shed tears, but they were blended with smiles and promises. Their slender fingers tenderly framed each other's faces as their foreheads touched, and thick glossy curls entwined when they whispered one more secret to each other, children again. A last farewell, and Theodora boarded with Drusus, waving to Antonia until she could no longer see the blazing red scarf her sister fluttered in return. They settled into their tented quarters to sleep through the return to Capri.

Hours later, the sea suddenly became turbulent. An enormous wave hoisted the boat, then released it, the vessel slamming down with a tearing groan. A mottled sky grew from the shore. Shouts from a nearby fleet became other vampyres, hurrying towards Pompeii and Herculaneum, frantically racing ships through the rough waters. Hestia drew alongside, and explained a vision she'd had the previous night—danger, heat, a blanket of steam and dust enveloping the coast. Then she froze and pointed eastward. Everyone turned to see a horrifying sight: Vesuvius had erupted, a black mushroom of smoke bloomed as fire scarred the sky for miles.

Many vampyres slept in the nearby towns; even more humans had begun their day. All were in danger. Theodora was beside herself, rushing to turn the boat around and join the others in their rescue mission. She gripped the rails as they raced against time, hair and chiton streaming behind her as waves hammered fiercely against the ship. Drusus leapt into the pit, gripping extra oars and pulling hard alongside the rowers. The closer they came to Pompeii, the thicker the dust and heat; boats passed them, full of human families in flight. Some were hurt, and cries of pain echoed across the water. Others choked their way through answers when questioned, their lungs burned from the gases.

The vampyres were informed of the past hours: an odd, gray morning, how the earth shuddered and convulsed, shattering amphoras of wine across tiled floors and upending lit braziers that quickly licked into fires. The widespread terror and confusion—*where are the children, the horses are screaming, what do we do, I cannot breathe, I cannot see*—had led to panic, releasing the primal side of survival. The city gates clogged with carts, animals, and bodies as a peppery rain of tiny, hot pumice began to fall, fueling a deeper wave of fear in the crowds. Some scrambled onto ships; others died falling beneath stampeding hooves or were crushed by the mindless mobs. Looters foraged through abandoned homes. One greedy slave owner capitalized on the situation and sold every slave he had to guard property for the rich. New masters fled to safety as these slaves were left behind.

Theodora knew who that must be.

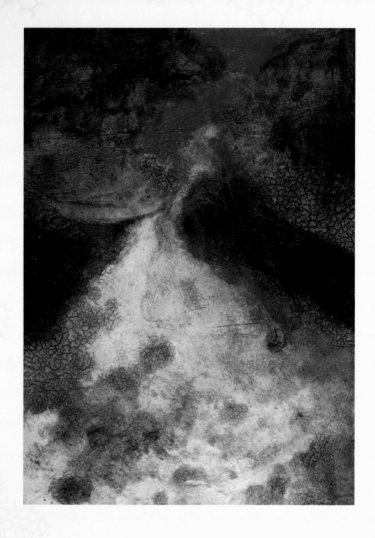

ABOVE: *The Wrath of Vesuvius*. 1st C. A.D. Fresco. Pompeii, Italy. From
the memory of a surviving vampyre. From The Pompeii Collection,
Hall of History, Venice, Italy.

The boats finally docked. The vampyres ripped bedding from the ship, then soaked it in the sea. They wrapped themselves for protection and pressed through the throng exiting the city.

Everything was heavily coated with dust and ricelike pellets; the heat was intense. The wise had escaped, while others peered through doorways, fearful of burns from the biting pumice. Nearby, a child screamed in the smoky gloom; sobs could be heard from within another shop. The vampyres fanned out, seeking friends and victims. Theodora called to Drusus to follow her to Antonia's bakery. Soon, they staggered into the still-erect building. A body lay there—the butcher, stabbed, a knife hilt protruding from his back. Theodora knelt and recognized a familiar bull carved into the hilt—Brutus. A strong foreboding flooded her limbs as she pieced together what had happened, telling Drusus, *"Brutus must have come for Antonia, and this man died in his attempt to protect her. They struggled... Brutus got what he wanted, but where are they? . . . the knife. The cave they worship in beneath the House of Mysteries. He has her . . . she is there . . . I feel her there. My sister is trapped in a cave with a madman, and he will never let her go."*

Theodora emerged from the bakery amid fresh cries for help from the nearby brothel. Other vampyres were struggling to pull humans towards the city gate when the ground heaved beneath them. A denser cloud roiled out of the volcano and spread through the streets. Another building groaned as its roof caved in from the deadly weight.

The cave was blocks away. They would never get there;

Antonia was doomed.

Surviving vampyres helped record the next events in Hestia's journal. It is stated that Theodora closed her eyes and stood, head bowed, in the center of the street, oblivious to warning shouts or the sizzle of stone pellets on her skin. Waves of power began to emanate from her as she slowly stretched her arms, palms forward, towards Vesuvius. Her eyes opened, her focus extending from the air before her and up the streets, through the city, past the hills, and into the heart of the monstrous volcano.

Everything in the path of her vision was arrested, frozen in whatever direction it had been going, locked in an arc or fall or flicker. Her chin lifted slightly, her eyes glazed, and the suspension broadened to cover the city. She closed her eyes, held herself as rigid as the statues lining the streets. Through the silence, Drusus heard her whisper, "*Hurry.*"

Vampyres behind her had stopped in astonishment as the wave she sent forth rolled out from the city. Her arms began to tremble with the effort, and they recognized what she offered. At inhuman speeds, their shapes tore holes through the ash-filled air, vacant tunnels appearing behind them. None of them had experienced anything like it, but they adapted immediately to the strange situation and, as they parted the atmosphere, saw it created a perfect retreat path. Drusus tore through the damaged streets, leaping over bodies, broken carts, and mounds of abandoned treasures, until he reached his destination. Forcing the door, he called for Antonia and heard a weak reply. He waded through the carnage, discovering a previously hidden door broken open from the heaving earth, and clambered his way down winding stairs. He gasped at the scene below: Antonia, tied upon an altar, the enormous statue of a bull having toppled across her. But still alive.

With a prayer to the Goddess, Drusus heaved and rocked the statue away, gently gathered the damaged body of his love's double, and staggered out of the cavern, back through the murky streets where Theodora stood.

In front of the bakery, Theodora's eyes remained closed, looking inward to command powerful waves and lock movement. It was here Brutus found her, exactly as he had hoped. The bait had been taken. Here was his chance to retrieve the other half of his matched pair. The butcher had nearly ruined his plan, but now! Withdrawing his knife from the body, Brutus smiled. *Theodora, you, too, are mine.*

The rope settled over her head and across her upper arms. He tried to pull it tight but was startled to find her as rigid as the marble columns of the city. Unfazed, Brutus slipped a rough hand behind her head and lifted his knife. *Mine. Mine . . .*

With a swift motion, he gouged a hole in her neck and plugged it with his lips as Drusus emerged from the dusty passageway with Antonia.

Jerked out of her trance, Theodora's eyes flew open to find Brutus wrapped around her, an insane leer pasted across his face. *"Now you are both mine. Always."*

Shocked, Theodora looked past him to see her sister's broken body held by Drusus. Inside of her, something tore, something she did not know could separate from her being. Instead of dealing with Brutus and retrieving her focus of Spirit to protect the searching rescuers, Theodora abandoned it all. Young and inexperienced in her gift, a red rage now consumed her, blurring her mind. She drew in the powers previously directed at the volcano, gathering them in a rush. Between gritted teeth, Theodora snarled at Brutus, *"Nia, watch me* NOW!" and flung her life force in hatred and horror at the man who would dare to harm her sister. Slowly, deliberately, Brutus was lifted high above the ground, where he began spinning, faster and faster. Then, an invisible push, and he flew backwards until, with a fleshy thud, his head split against a marble statue. His body sagged downwards, twitching, leaving a grim trail to the base of the monument where he sat upright against the wall below. The falling ash regained its reign over Pompeii, showering Brutus, coating him immediately. There he remained for eternity: legs splayed, mouth open—as Vesuvius claimed his form as its own.

Theodora collapsed in the street. The angry crater blasted its contents into the sky. Roofs caved, walls toppled—Hell had arrived.

With the last of his warrior strength, Drusus heaved her body upon his other shoulder. He blindly stumbled towards the city gate, feeling the heat as pumice kernels relentlessly fell. Finally, helping hands appeared and they reached the ship. Rowers heaved frantically to exit the deadly shore, pulling for their lives, and the exhausted survivors sailed to Capri.

Vampyres on the boat administered as best they could to

the three—bodies were rinsed, mouths cleared, eyes wiped. As Hestia gently washed the grime from Theodora's face, she started, then blinked several times. Theodora's sapphire tattoos had disappeared from her brow. There was no explanation; even experienced Vampyre healers had no idea what it meant.

The healers did recognize one thing, however: Antonia was beyond their skills. Broken back and ribs, crushed hips, and more: the ash coated her lungs, weakening her body by the minute. Each breath was obvious agony; she moaned in her unconscious state. Drusus was beside himself. Hoping to restore her, he tore his own wrists open to force blood between her lips. She roused, but the respite was brief.

Lying next to Theodora, Antonia turned her head and, with dull eyes, found her twin. She groaned but still reached out to weave their fingertips together, then her eyes closed again. Antonia whispered, "Wait . . . for me."

Then she was still.

Awash in grief and driven by fear, Drusus fell to his knees before Hestia. "NO! This cannot happen, I cannot lose Theodora as well, I cannot bear it! In Pompeii, she released her power against the slave trader. Now, she is not dead, yet not alive! How can this be? My love has no mark on her, yet she is gone; and where?"

Hestia knew Nyx as a great power, fueled by the spirit world. However, the physical world has its own rules, and even a goddess cannot always command them. The Change makes vampyres near timeless, but not invincible.

A painful lesson.

Hestia considered a moment, then nodded. *"Drusus, there is a way, but it is shrouded in mystery . . . unpredictable. I can only try."*

The vampyres of Capri gathered around a large table. From within an elaborately embroidered bag, Hestia poured ten marble stones, so white they glowed. Each had a crudely carved rune in the center. She said, *"These are ancient, from a source no one knows or understands. They are recognized by the Goddess, but not of the Goddess; they come from a Prophetess who existed long before our history was recorded."*

Eyes closed, she entered a trance, her arms rising, her body rocking to and fro. She spoke in a long-forgotten tongue, calling upon nameless forces to join her.

And they answered.

An other-worldly voice emerged from her lips.

> *"Drusus, Son of Erebus, Warrior to Theodora, you must release yourself to find her. You must destroy yourself to save her. You must surrender yourself to return her."*

She opened her eyes and traced a circle on the table before Drusus, then a star to contain it. She gathered the stones, holding each aloft, allowing the threads of silver veins to reflect the candlelight before returning them to the bag. She held it open to him.

"Drusus, allow the stones within to find your hand as you take them from the bag. Center one stone on each separate arc of the circle." He followed her instructions, withdrawing and placing, leaving

five stones in the bag. "*Now, allow the remaining stones to find you as well, and place them above the original set, toward each point.*" Once the stones were paired, Hestia studied them carefully and drew a breath.

"*Drusus, with the questions we have asked the powers, I can only hope to understand these answers.*" She pointed to a rune stone with a barren tree on its face, just above one with a spiral that thickened towards its center. "*Theodora's soul has fractured, branched away. Her energies maintain her life above the ground, as does a tree, but they also flow where we do not see, taking her to the roots of her soul. She nears Nyx's realm in the Otherworld, but she is not whole. It is only through a spirit journey that you might find her branches and draw them together.*" She indicated another pair of stones. "*And here is the Bridge, where journeys converge. All crossings are challenging; some are allowed but once, offering no return. Here, it is paired with Spirit; this is where a decision will be made.*" Hestia saw the dangers indicated in the other three pairings and their placement on the circle, but stopped there.

Drusus was Theodora's warrior; here lay his task.

Hestia's shoulders sagged. "*Drusus, this path is one you must forge without the confines of your body. There is great risk here. To leave your body and travel on the energy of your spirit threatens both life forces: the seen and the unseen.*"

He shook his head. "*I must go. Hurry, show me this path; every moment takes her farther away from me.*"

Tears welled in Hestia's eyes to see the desperation in his face. She took his hand and said, "*I have a poison. Too much will kill a vampyre, but in small, constant doses, it will hold your body sus-*

pended and free your mind. This is a terrible risk; I must take care in administering each dose. But I will do this. Drusus, I fear it is wrong, but I will do this."

The vial was fetched and Antonia's body tenderly carried away. Drusus lay in her place, beside his love, holding Theodora's hand. Hestia uncorked the bottle. With the utmost care, she allowed the smallest drop to escape and fall between his lips.

At first, it was as if a new power was exploring his form, adjusting to its nooks and crannies, testing each muscle group for strength and flexibility as he flexed and shuddered. Suddenly, his body went rigid, a spasm locking it in place as a bloom began at his lips and broken blood vessels spread across his face. The vampyres, confused, looked to Hestia for guidance. She placed a hand over his heart, and said, *"He is on the journey. We will wait."*

She stayed beside him, refusing sustenance, to maintain the poisonous doses. At times, his muscles would suddenly twitch, or he would moan and mutter jumbled phrases. As the days wore on, his face took on a painful grimace, his jaws locked and lips pulled back in agony.

After five days, Hestia could bear no more. Although exhausted, she gathered the vampyres and cast a Circle around him, hoping to somehow transfer their remaining strength to the warrior. For a moment, it appeared to work. His features relaxed; his furrowed brow smoothed. Then, Drusus opened his eyes and searched about himself, seeking but not seeing.

"No, Theodora, don't cross! Don't join her! I'm here, can't you hear

me call? Theodora!"

A primal scream erupted from him as he was jerked upright, like an enormous hook had slipped under his sternum to lift him forward. He turned his face and realized where he was. His hand extending to her, he said, *"Hestia, help me . . . ."*

She shook her head. *"There is no more I can do."* She held up the vial. *"Your body cannot tolerate any more of this."*

And to her horror, he ripped it out of her hand. Before Hestia could respond, Drusus had upended the bottle in his mouth. His head snapped back, his arms fell away from his body, and as the blood burst through his skin, coating his body, he choked out, *"Theodora . . ."*

Then the unseen force released him as the vampyres rushed forward. Hestia placed her hand on his chest, and knew.

Drusus, too, was gone.

Hestia turned to where Theodora lay and gasped. No longer merely pale, she was almost . . . *transparent.* As the life force drained from each cell, her body released the last traces of spirit held captive for those past days. The shattered soul of their young priestess was gone forever.

The pair lay, fingertips touching, like marble carvings above a tomb—equally beautiful, equally cold. The vampyres slid loving fingers across each forehead, touching where a crescent once glowed, then over eternally silent lips, and down to touch the center of each chest, where a heart once beat. Fists clasped across their chests, eyes closed, in unison they bid the lovers to *"Merry meet again."*

The Farewell Ritual held by Vampyres, while rare, is a

ceremony of aching beauty, infused with raw grief for a loss. Anyone can imagine how it felt for the vampyres of Capri during the full moon that month. The pain they carried grew; the shadows prevailed, no one could ignore it. Hestia publicly rent her clothes and tore her hair in despair, issuing the famous statement:

> *"Like an obscene, drunken villain, Vesuvius has vomited destruc-*
> *tion upon our beloved Pompeii and Herculaneum. The unique*
> *beauty, grace, and spirit of these two magical cities will never be*
> *duplicated. We are unable to remain here, in Capri, as we cannot*
> *bear to be near their desecrated corpses. By formal edict the Vam-*
> *pyre High Council will, henceforth, make our home elsewhere."*

The palace was sold.

The pilgrimage begun.

You might believe that, placed in Theodora's situation, you would have had the strength or power to make better choices. None of us knows, Fledgling, how we may be . . . until we are there. Some of it will be up to you, some will come from the love sent by the Goddess, and the rest will be how time unfolds within the circumstances.

But know this: You have been Chosen, and everything happens for a purpose.

As for the journey, the remaining vampyres of Capri joined the High Council in a search for a home. They settled in Florence, initiating an artistic fervor there that some still believe to be unrivaled at any other time in human history.

But as the years passed and the power of Rome grew more in-trusive, our ancestors began looking for a more remote, more acceptable home.

In April of 421 A.D., the Vampyre High Priestess Torcellia was traveling from Florence to northern Italy when she dis-covered an intriguing settlement that was being constructed by humans trying to escape barbarian invasions. This settle-ment was being built directly on a system of manmade islands

ABOVE: *Capri: from the Palace Rooftop.* 1st C. A.D. Fresco. A farewell study painted for Hestia prior to the exodus of the vampyres.

OPPOSITE: Gold ducat, 14th. C. commemorative coin issued in honor of the philanthropy shown by the High Council of Vampyres to the city of Venice.

surrounded by lagoons. Torcellia instantly felt a kinship with the humans, as well as the idea of building a world meant to be a fortress against outsiders, and she put the strength and wealth, talent, and ingenuity of vampyre society behind the venture.

The struggling humans embraced her help, so much so that in 639 A.D., the last act of Torcellia's long life was to commission the building of the Palazzo Ducale, known today as the Doge's Palace, for the human nobility that had shown her such acceptance and kindness.

Directly across the murky Mediterranean, situated so that Torcellia could sit and gaze upon the lustrous city that would eventually be called Venice, the High Priestess built a fabulous island of her own, where she decreed the Vamypre High Council had finally, after centuries of restlessness and longing for the sea, found its permanent home. She named

the island San Clemente, after the Warrior who had bound himself to her four centuries before, just after she Changed.

Today, Fledgling, we do indeed make our ancestral home, the site of our beloved Vampyre High Priestess and our governing Council, on San Clemente Island, which adorns the Mediterranean, like an exquisite pearl, just off the coast of Venice.

Much, much more about our culture exists in the halls of San Clemente's Museum of Vampyre History, found below

the rooms of our High Council; the most sacred of our ritual processes as well as interpretations of vampyre evolution are found in the Sanctuary of Nyx, another branch of studies you will encounter in the House of Night.

As you progress through your years at the House of Night, you will learn more of our High Council. At this time it is important only to understand that we are ruled by one benevolent High Priestess, who is voted into power by the entire body of vampyres. Our High Priestess answers only to the Vampyre High Council, consisting of seven Priestesses who are chosen by the seven national vampyre districts, and are revered for their wisdom and devotion to our Goddess.

ABOVE: *Blessed Be.* 2010. A common exercise on San Clemente Island is to walk the mist at dusk. Photograph courtesy of the High Council of Vampyres, Venice, Italy.

These eight magnificent vampyres are eternally protected by our warriors, the Sons of Erebus. So be at peace, Fledgling, our High Priestess resides over our Council, and all is right in the world.

ABOVE: *The Portal.* 2010. As one door closes, another opens; fledglings will discover enlightenment and power in their lives through the guidance of Nyx. Photograph courtesy of the High Council of Vampyres, Venice, Italy.

And I begin...

Fledgling, this book is meant as a reference throughout your first year in a House of Night. We encourage you to document your growth physically, emotionally and spiritually.

This page is intended for you to record how you see the world at this moment. It is your beginning as a Third Former.

This page is intended for you to record how you see the world as you leave the Labyrinth behind and enter your second year in the House of Night. The Wings of Eros await you.

ABOVE: *Haus der Nacht*, Frankfurt, Germany, 1085 A.D. Nyx
exists in every star, and is reflected in every cycle of the moon.

CHAPTER FIVE
Words of Hope from Fellow Fledglings

THOUGH YOU MAY BE feeling afraid and confused, you are far from the first fledgling to experience the life-changing, exciting event of being newly Marked. For thousands of years human teenagers have been Marked. You are not alone. Those who have gone before you understand your fears. They would have you be strong and steadfast, young fledgling! The following quotes are words of wisdom from famous vampyres throughout the ages explaining how they felt when they were first Marked:

ABOVE: CHANDOS. c. 1589 A.D. Through an infrared lens, a vampyre photographer was able to capture a compelling glimpse of the original of this painting. Shakespeare's tattoos were later obscured by a jealous consort. The defacing brushwork also receded his hairline and aged him over the initial masterpiece. The altered painting was sold to the National Portrait Gallery of London where it hangs today.

" 'Tis truth made more pure
by fear and pain, though if 'twas
possible I would cry, 'Dark Lady!
Mark me again… again…' "

—WILLIAM SHAKESPEARE
Playwright

ABOVE: The Brygos Painter, ca. 470 B.C.E. The poet holds a harp on the side of a Grecian urn. From the Greco-Roman Museum of Night History.

"When I remember that moment,
then I can speak no more,
but my tongue falls silent,
and at once a delicate flame
courses beneath my skin,
and with my eyes I see nothing,
and my ears hum,
and a wet sweat bathes me,
and a trembling seizes me all over."

—SAPPHO

Vampyre Poet Laureate, Ancient Greece

ABOVE: Rome, Italy. 1st C. B.C.E. Marble. Cicero encouraged the sculptor to age him; it was rumored his sophisticated letters were often discounted as plagiarized once he was met in person due to his youthful looks.

"I follow Nyx as the surest guide,
and resign myself,
with implicit obedience,
to Her sacred ordinances."

—CICERO
Roman Philosopher

ABOVE: Tibet. 18th C. embroidered silk (thangka). Photograph by permission of the Himalayan Regional HON, Tibet.

"At that instant I became
a blooming lotus flower.
The water in which I flourished
was a single teardrop
from Nyx."

—GREEN TARA
Tibetan High Priestess

ABOVE: Salem, Massachusetts. 17th C. woodcut. Used by permission of Early American Literary Society, MA.

"In the midst of darkness and
decay and fear my Mark was a
beautiful sapphire beacon,
lending me strength and leading me
to freedom and to Nyx."

—SARAH OSBORNE
*Marked in 1692 while jailed
during the Salem witch trials.*

ABOVE: *Shekinah.* Always an artist, Shekinah cast her own death mask as a fledgling. After completing the Change, she placed the cast upon her face and felt a strange warmth against her forehead. Upon removing the mask, she was astonished to discover her newly filled crescent had etched itself into the plaster form. Photograph by permission of the Vampyre Hall of High Priestesses, Venice, Italy.

"Was I filled with fear,
uncertainty, and trepidation
the day I was Marked? Of course.
But soon I learned fear can be
overcome by faith;
uncertainty can lead to new
beginnings, and trepidation can be
vanquished by confidence.
Being Marked is truly about the
magick of possibilities..."

—SHEKINAH
High Priestess of Vampyres

So, Fledgling, we hope the conclusion of this handbook finds you more informed and, thusly, more confident as you begin the new life path of a fledgling at the House of Night. Remember that you are not alone, and that countless fledglings have traveled the road that stretches before you. Look to your mentor for advice and guidance, to your fellow fledglings for companionship, and to Nyx for solace from the uncertainties that lie before you.

We leave you with a poetic prayer, written in a style that has become known, even in the human world, as a Shakespearean sonnet. Shakespeare was once standing where you are today, at the precipice of one of life's greatest and most magickal adventures. We wish you always, to blessed be . . .

THE FLEDGLING SONNET

May Nyx's blessings find you strong and sure
Steadfast you shall be ev'n should fear betray
Though days turn dark and endless nights endure
With sweet love our Goddess will guide your way

Listen not to whispers; those thoughts deny
Death is not proud, nor does he rule your life
He is dust swept clean when Nyx hears you cry
Atropos cuts him with a goddess knife

Don't hearken to Death; instead embrace Hope
She is sister to Nyx, more near — more true
And then greet Joy, steadfast she'll help you cope
Dearest Marked one, we all rejoice in you

With this prayer begone! Sadness, fear, and pain
Merry meet...part...and merry meet again!

Also by P. C. Cast

Marked

Betrayed

Chosen

Untamed

Hunted

Tempted

Burned